The Box Of Souls

Family Relics Book 1

by

Tanya Miranda

The Box of Souls
By Tanya Miranda

Cover by Seedlings Design Studio
www.seedlingsonline.com

Published by Blue Dragonfly Publishing
www.bluedragonflypublishing.com

ISBN-13: 978-0692477526
ISBN-10: 0692477527

For Ryan & Roman,
the joys of my life.

AWARENESS

Jasmyn is a deep sleeper. Loud commotions like fire alarms, thunderstorms, or even earthquakes rarely wake her, but tonight a gentle voice interrupts her dreams. A succession of soft whispers slowly crescendos until she awakens and sits upright in her bed with beads of sweat streaming down her neck. *Who called my name?* Her eyes dart about her bedroom, finding everything as it should be. *There's no one here.* After several breaths, Jasmyn moves to the edge of her bed and plants her bare feet flat on the floor. *I must have been dreaming.*

A beam of moonlight shines diagonally across her room, charting a path to her window. The crisp evening breeze brushes against her cheeks as she pulls gold and silver starburst-patterned curtains aside. The moon shines so brightly that it enchants Jasmyn for a few seconds before she looks over to the digital alarm clock on her nightstand—it's two in the morning.

Someone whispers her name again, or at least Jasmyn thinks she hears a voice. It seems dreamlike, as if it wasn't a voice at all but a whooshing current of air, coaxing her forward, leading her toward her bedroom door. She follows it eagerly, cautiously.

After taking a quick peek down the hallway, she tiptoes to her sister's room, creeping up to the white bedside table, almost knocking over the pink ceramic piggy bank. She gently pokes Katarina's shoulder, but her little sister continues sleeping. She sneaks across the paisley-patterned hallway rug to her brother's room and walks past his pig-like snoring. Two similar guttural sounds emanate from her parents' bedroom the next door down. *Everyone is asleep.*

The whisper, the pull, draws Jasmyn to her grandmother's bedroom at the end of the hallway. Her grandmother's window is wide open, allowing the brisk night air inside. The wind blows the sheer white curtain up and away so it falls fluidly down to a lifeless state, then rises back up again. The bottom half curves upwards into a slow-moving wave, like an index finger signaling her to come inside. The moonlight illumines a straight path along the hardwood floor, toward her grandmother's bed, the source of the call. Jasmyn inches forward.

The tall white bookshelf along her grandmother's wall calls her attention. The small intricate boxes, the wrought iron miniature statues, the wooden figurines, all of her grandmother's antique treasures seem to emanate mild pulses toward Jasmyn. She doesn't know how to interpret the vibrations; she only knows the surge is there in the room, originating from the shelf, directed right at her, almost juddering against her skin. She presses on, sending the pulses to the back of her mind and focusing on the pull that now seems to tug her toward her grandmother.

At the bedside, she gazes down upon her grandmother's peaceful expression and recalls when taking afternoon naps with her was a daily event. When she was younger, before her sister was born, when Jasmyn was the center of her grandmother's world, they would spend hours together telling stories, drawing, painting, and pretending to do magic. These days, she barely spends any time with her grandmother. Katarina is now, and has been for a long time, her grandmother's favorite.

Jasmyn presses her eyes shut. *Stop that. Forget about that. That was a long time ago.*

She returns to studying her grandmother's serene face. The deep creases of her grandmother's years flow across her forehead and down the sides of her cheeks. Laugh lines border a slight smile. Her pearl-white wavy locks drape over the butterflies printed on her nightgown, each strand bending in perfect crescent shapes as if groomed by a professional stylist. Jasmyn's eyes follow the curls down her arms and continue toward her hands folded over her stomach.

Just as she is about to reach for her grandmother's hand, the vibrations suddenly stop. An unnerving silence covers the room so all she hears is her own breath, her own heartbeat. She notices her grandmother's eerily still form and places the back of her wrist just over her nose in search of some flow of air. There is none.

Gasping, Jasmyn pulls her hand away from her grandmother's face and presses it against her own chest before stepping backwards and rushing to her parents' bedroom.

COVENHOOD

In a luxurious duplex apartment in New York City, overlooking the breadth of Central Park, Patricia awakens to a sickening sensation she hasn't felt since the last witch of her coven died one hundred twenty-seven years ago. "Agatha," she whispers into the night. Sitting up in her king size bed with arms wrapped around bent knees, she allows streams of tears to make their way down to her red satin bed sheets. The drowning feeling in the pit of her stomach and the spasms traveling through her body are bearable but temporarily crippling. She breathes deeply and waits for it to pass, as it has done so many times before. When a witch dies, a little bit of each surviving sister witch dies with her. It's a natural part of the sisterhood bond; a part Patricia knows all too well.

In an attempt to take her mind off the debilitating ailments, Patricia recalls the last time she saw Agatha—the day Agatha's son was born. As Agatha held her newborn son in her arms, him struggling to latch onto her nipple, her trying to figure out the best breastfeeding method, she accused Patricia of being careless about hiding her magic. It wasn't the first time they'd had this argument, but Agatha made sure it was the last.

Patricia, as always, was defiant of any suggestion that she change her way of life. Her attitude was something Agatha had suffered through decades, centuries, across cities, countries, and continents. Patricia's actions had required them to move from their homes time and time again, disappearing before authorities came to question them about 'suspicious activity' reported by the neighbors. She lacked Agatha's subtlety and the desire to be part of a community, to live a normal life. Agatha wanted to plant roots. Patricia wanted to fly freely at will. Life changed for Agatha when she met Elliot and got married. She shed her immortality to give birth to a son. Moving and restarting her life was no longer an option. She had a family to think about. Roots were planted, without Patricia's approval.

"Patricia," Agatha said, cradling her newborn, "if you won't hide your powers, if you won't live a normal life, you can't be a part of mine. Elliot and Kevin are my life now."

"And our life together, all these years..." Patricia swallowed hard as she tried to maintain a courageous face, "means nothing to you?"

Gazing down at her son, with her index finger stuck in the squeeze of his tiny, full-handed grip, Agatha shook her head. "It's amazing how the birth of a child changes you, like a switch has been turned off in me in some ways and turned on in others. My life is no longer my own. It belongs to him now—to them." Agatha raised her eyes toward Patricia as she hardened her tone. "If you wish to continue living the way you do, spewing magic without caution, flaunting your powers without caring how it will affect my family… without considering how it will hurt my son... then our time together has come to an end."

Feeling abandoned by her lifelong friend, Patricia straightened her back and pressed her lips together in defiance. "Very well," she said, her throat tightening as she swallowed. Before losing her composure, Patricia turned on her heel and walked out of the hospital room and out of Agatha's life.

That was sixty-three years ago; sixty-three years since Patricia last saw her sister witch. The awful memory aches in Patricia's heart as she lies back down in her bed. She never understood why a witch would give up immortality for a child and a limited lifespan, but she knows all witches eventually do. Finna was over four hundred years old when she gave birth to Agatha and lived another thirty years before old age took her. Agatha was three hundred years old when she gave birth to her son. Patricia is almost four hundred years old and has never felt the need. Although the natural desire to procreate is strong, and grows stronger as a witch's immortal years pass and generations of her relatives die of old age before her eyes, leaving her with no one to call family, it has yet to spark within Patricia. She's not ready to settle down and give up her freedom, her powers, her immortality, and is convinced that no one will ever be worthy of such a sacrifice.

"We were immortal, you fool," she whispers, wiping the tears from her chin as Agatha's last words echo in her head. *Our time together has come to an end.* "Your children better be worth it."

With nausea and a headache still lingering, Patricia jumps out of bed and paces back and forth across her living room floor, going through a mental list of the things she needs to do. The sun's early morning light shines through the panoramic windows of her apartment and clarifies Patricia's priorities. Her tasks are simple: Secure the *Book of Whispers*, gather Agatha's relics, and find her successor.

After spending a good hour searching for Agatha's family online and finding only an address in San Francisco for Elliot McKeery, Agatha's husband, Patricia throws her hands up and closes her laptop. *Time for some good old-fashioned magic.*

With her hands shifting left and right over a crystal bowl full of water, Patricia tosses in a few ingredients, including sugar, salt, fresh codfish eyes, and a piece of cloth from a white lacy sweater she took from Agatha before she got married. She holds up a picture of Agatha and herself during their single days, a black-and-white photo from the '30s, and recites a spell to display Agatha's children.

In the crimping waves, she sees the grown-up face of Agatha's son and gasps when the realization hits her. His day-old stubble, the gray peppered through his hair, and the laugh lines around the corners of his eyes embody the time passed between her and her sister witch. *If Kevin is this old, what must Agatha look like?* The thought of a wrinkly, weathered Agatha creates a shock that circulates throughout Patricia's body.

"No daughters," Patricia whispers as the images in the water fade into clarity. She holds up a worn-out picture of Agatha and her newborn son—one Agatha had sent to try and reconcile with Patricia shortly after their disagreement. Patricia recites the spell again, this time aimed at Kevin's children, hoping to find a granddaughter to which Agatha passed on the gift.

In the water she sees a teenage girl with long, wavy, auburn hair and pronounced eyes, arguing with Kevin in a car. "Jasmyn," Patricia whispers as the name comes to her, "eighteen years old." In the vision, Jasmyn slams the car door shut and takes a deep breath to calm her face before casually walking into the house as if she wasn't angry just moments earlier. "Tough kid," Patricia says as the image weakens.

She then sees Kevin at a soccer match with a son who scores the game-winning goal. "Logan... sixteen years old," Patricia whispers. Through the swirling water, Patricia sees Kevin tickling a little girl with auburn hair tied in a ponytail and bangs hovering just over her glasses. The little girl's grin reveals two big buckteeth that make Patricia smile. "Katarina, eight years old," she says with a sigh.

To conjure more scenes of the three children with their father, hoping to find one that includes one of them conducting some magic, Patricia dips her hand into the bowl and recites another spell. No such image appears.

From her concoctions, Patricia cannot see which granddaughter Agatha chose as her successor, or if Agatha chose to let her magic die with her as she had always claimed she would. After an impatient sigh, Patricia realizes her next task—she is going to San Francisco to meet Agatha's family.

~ ~ ~

Regina doesn't know what to think of the sudden bout of nausea forcing her into a tight fetal position in the middle of her bed. Nearly two centuries of immortal existence and never has Regina felt as sick as she does now, except for the day her mother died.

But it isn't just the nausea that concerns her, nor her muscles throbbing, nor her body trembling from a cold sweat; it's the random images of Agatha spinning inside her head that are unsettling. After keeping her nausea at bay for just a few minutes longer, as she shuffles through unexpected memories of her sister witch, Regina heads straight to her bathroom to throw up.

Hours after her cheek found a relatively comfortable position on the cool marble tiles on the bathroom floor, with tears and saliva dried on her chin and in the folds of her long red hair, the sound of her cell phone wakes her. Regina squints toward the dim rays of sunlight shining through the window blinds. *Who would possibly call me this early in the morning?* A cramp forms in her stomach when she pushes herself up to kneel over the toilet. Vertigo takes hold the instant she rises to her feet and sends her equilibrium into a spin. She grabs the bathroom's doorframe to hold herself up and, a couple of clumsy footsteps later, finally makes it to her bed. She takes one last deep breath before shutting her eyes and surrendering to a long, deep sleep.

3

MEMORABILIA

After consoling Katarina most of the morning, Kevin and his wife Paula spend the afternoon making arrangements for Agatha's wake tomorrow. Logan tries to watch television with his little sister, but after blankly staring at the screen, the two eventually fall asleep. Alone in her room, Jasmyn attempts to watch television, cries, sleeps, and writes in her journal.. Her door has been closed for most of the day.

As twilight approaches, Logan stands up from the living room couch and stretches his arms out and upwards. He tugs on the purple and pink wool blanket wrapped around Katarina, the same blanket Agatha stitched before Katarina was born, and wakes her up. A sleepy Katarina pulls it back, bundling the worn edges up under a tight hug. Jinx, their mini golden retriever, growls up at Logan.

"You won't be able to go to sleep later tonight if you keep napping." Logan attempts another tug, "Let's do something together."

"I don't want to do anything."

"We've been sleeping and vegging all afternoon."

"But... I feel sad."

"I know, Kat, but maybe you'll feel better if we do something. Keeping your mind busy will help you stop thinking about being sad. Come on."

"Like what?" Katarina asks, pouting.

Her pitiful face squeezes Logan's heart, and he sighs. "If

Nana were alive right now, and everything were normal, and you could do anything in the world, what would it be?"

"I'd sit with Nana so she could read me a story from her book," Katarina says. Her pink, swollen eyes follow the blanket's stitch pattern that switches between shades of pink and purple.

Logan smiles softly. "Okay. Let's go get her book."

He takes Katarina's hand, pulls her up and out of the blanket's hold, and heads up the stairs to their grandmother's room. Just before opening the door, Katarina pulls back on Logan's hand. "Wait. She's not in there... is she?"

"No Kat. She's not in there anymore. It's okay to go inside."

"But..." Katarina's eyes begin to moisten.

Logan kneels down in front of his little sister. "Kat, if you don't want to go inside, it's okay. Tell me what the book looks like, and I'll find it for you."

"No, I'll go in." Katarina inhales deeply and blows a long burst of air through narrowed lips. "I can do it."

With her hand in his, Logan leads Katarina into their grandmother's bedroom. Jinx immediately jumps up onto Agatha's bed and lies on his side on the pillows.

Along the dresser is their grandmother's jewelry box displaying her many antique necklaces, pendants, and charms. Katarina is drawn to the sparkling gems. "I've always loved Nana's jewelry." She stares down at a ruby amulet. After fumbling through rings, bracelets, and brooches holding a variety of colored stones, Katarina sees a round, steel medallion with a black dragon etched on its face. The other pieces in her hands slide back into the jewelry box as Katarina lifts the pendant up to her eyes for a closer inspection. Although she found all of her grandmother's trinkets pretty, this medallion is not like the others. It doesn't glimmer. Rather, it's made of steel, and its round edges are worn and dented. On the face is a dragon etching stained black; flames burst from the dragon's snout, and its jagged tail curls down and then upwards in front of it, forming a round border along the medallion's edge. She flips it to see more etchings on the other side that look like words from the *Book of Whispers*.

Katarina's eyes focus on the black stain of the dragon's tail. *I wonder why Nana never wore this. She loved wearing her necklaces. Maybe it's special. Maybe she hid it for a reason. I should put it back. But it's so pretty. Maybe someone gave it to her. Maybe she made it. Maybe—*

"Why don't you put it on?" Logan asks, interrupting Katarina's thoughts.

"Are you sure it's okay?"

"Mom and Dad wouldn't mind."

Katarina looks at the medallion and then back at Logan. "What if Nana wanted Jaz to have it?"

"Jaz will understand."

Katarina raises her eyebrows, questioning Logan's claim.

"I'll make Jaz understand. Let's put it on."

As he ties the medallion's black thread chain around Katarina's neck, Logan wonders how Jasmyn will react to any of this. He understands Katarina's fear, having witnessed his older sister's jealousy and even scolded her for her behavior. He's also seen the preferential treatment Katarina receives from his parents that fuels Jasmyn's fire and has given her reason to act out. But now isn't the time to give Katarina pep talks about tolerance and forgiveness or to give Jasmyn leeway for a one-sided upbringing; his baby sister is suffering, and Logan wants to do anything to keep her from crying.

"Just tell Jaz that it makes you feel better and that you want to share it with her."

Katarina nods, feeling a surge of warmth enter her body.

She closes her eyes for a moment and can almost feel her grandmother's arms hugging her.

On the dark wooden console standing below the windowsill, Katarina finds the *Book of Whispers*. She lifts it with a slight grunt and wedges the thick book under her armpit before walking over to her grandmother's bookshelf. She notices a small wooden box—it makes no sound when she shakes it near her ear.

"Is there anything in there?" Logan asks.

Katarina shrugs her shoulders. "It sounds empty."

"Do you want to take it to your room?"

"Can I?" Katarina asks with a hint of happiness in her voice.

"Sure."

"Can I take a few more things?"

"If it makes you feel better."

After spending a few hours going through almost everything in their grandmother's room, Logan and Katarina walk down to the kitchen with a cardboard box full of their grandmother's belongings. They had gathered several small jars of stones, salts, metals, and crystals that can compare to those found in museum galleries, a few stone statues of flowers, incense sticks, candle holders, a couple wooden boxes, several strands of jewelry, and of course, the *Book of Whispers*.

It's close to ten at night, and Jasmyn is eating a cold turkey sandwich at the granite kitchen counter when Logan sets the box on the table. Dark circles weigh heavy under her eyes, and her nose is pink and raw. Logan notices her disheveled hair and realizes he hasn't seen his older sister all day. He wonders if his parents have consoled Jasmyn the way they spent hours with Katarina this morning. He's fairly certain they haven't.

He offers Jasmyn some milk before pouring himself a glass. "How are you holding up?"

"Fine, I guess." Jasmyn glances at the cardboard box. "What's all that?" she asks after taking a bite.

"I thought it would make Kat feel better if we went through Nana's stuff."

The soft shine of the dragon medallion around Katarina's neck glimmers in Jasmyn's direction. She stops chewing and swallows the half-chewed food in a loud gulp, trying to keep her face from turning red, wanting to scream but holding it in as she's learned to do since she was ten, since the day Katarina came home from the hospital, only a few days old, and dominated her family's affection. Despite her attempt to maintain control, her emotions surge to the surface and materialize in tears in her eyes and redness in her cheeks. She remembers how the medallion used to hang lazily from her grandmother's neck when she would read her bedtime stories and how her grandmother swore she could have it when she was older. It is an heirloom, with a history that was promised to Jasmyn before Katarina was born, and now Katarina has taken it, like she has taken so many other things. She took her place in the family. She has hoarded her parents' affection, stolen her brother's alliance, and now she holds the one thing that reminds her of the grandmother who used to dote on her and no one else.

Logan notices Jasmyn glaring at Katarina. "What's wrong?"

"She was my grandmother too, you know."

The crack in Jasmyn's voice gives away her pain, but Logan is already on Katarina's defense. He speaks softly so Katarina cannot hear. "Kat's been crying all day. I thought it would make her feel better to get the book she used to read with Nana. She saw a few things in Nana's room. I told her it was okay to take them."

I've been crying too! I miss Nana too, damn it! Jasmyn

14

takes a deep breath and shoots an enraged glare at Katarina and then back at Logan. After another breath, she whispers back, "Of course."

Logan rolls his eyes and shakes his head as he lets out a long exhale.

"Do you want the medallion, Jaz?" Katarina asks, her voice almost trembling. "We can share it."

"Keep it. It's just a stupid medallion from a stupid story."

"There's a story behind it?" Katarina asks with wide, hopeful eyes.

Because Katarina and Logan excluded Jasmyn from their hunt for comforting treasures, she decides not to share the medallion story with her younger siblings. She feels a bittersweet sense of satisfaction at finally having something of her own, something she doesn't have to share with, or surrender to, Katarina. It will be her secret.

Without another word Jasmyn glares at both Logan and Katarina and exits the kitchen to return to her bedroom.

~ ~ ~

After Logan explains to Katarina that Jasmyn's abrupt behavior is her way of dealing with their grandmother's death, he finally convinces his little sister to read a story from the *Book of Whispers*, as they had planned. He walks past a slumped Katarina to the kitchen table to pull the enormous book out of the cardboard box. He hands it to his little sister.

Katarina has always been fascinated by the book's intricately woven leather cover with the detailed emblem in its center. She stares at the cover for a few moments, remembering the times she had to hold the book up for her grandmother because her grandmother's arms were too weak. She recalls the range of voices her grandmother used when acting out different roles and the way she would always end the stories with, "and all was right with the world, as it usually is in the world of magic."

Katarina wonders if her grandmother ever shared these stories with Jasmyn since she never saw Jasmyn and her grandmother talk the way she and her grandmother used to. *She must have. How else would Jaz know about a medallion story?*

"Logan, what's a green fog?"

Perplexed, Logan shakes his head. "I don't understand the question."

"Nana once said Jasmyn's heart is blinded by a green fog, and that's why she doesn't sit with Nana to read stories anymore."

"Oh." Logan raises his head with a half-smile. "She meant Jasmyn was jealous. The green fog represents jealousy, like the green monster."

"Jealous of what?" Katarina raises her eyebrows.

Logan has dreaded the day Katarina would look to him to explain the source of Jasmyn's behavior. Although his parents claim Jasmyn's sensitivity is prototypical teenage drama, Logan has always maintained that Jasmyn isn't entirely to blame for her temperament. The thought of choosing a side between his older and younger sisters has never crossed his mind, so Logan attempts to lay out a neutral depiction of the entire situation. "Nana thought Jasmyn was jealous of you, but Jasmyn was never really jealous—at least I never thought so. She was probably hurt because everyone stopped showing her affection. So she started acting out. Her behavior has gotten worse as she's gotten older, and she has become colder and more private. Nana, Mom, and Dad just refer to Jasmyn's behavior as jealousy because it's easy. But it's way more complicated than that. Trust me."

"So the green fog is still around?"

Logan smiles softly at his little sister's angelic eyes. "Yes, it's still around."

Katarina nods confidently as if Logan stated an indisputable fact, though she doesn't quite understand its full meaning. He is, after all, her big brother, and whenever Logan says, "trust me," she does.

With an eight-year-old child's unquenchable desire for wonder, Katarina places the *Book of Whispers* on the kitchen table and pulls out the small wooden box she took from her grandmother's shelf. A large ring with dirty, rusty skeleton keys follows. Her fingertips caress the bullet circles along the sides of the wooden box. The edges are lined with a continuous metal strip that ends at a tiny iron lock with a key opening.

While Katarina plays with her grandmother's antiques, Logan prepares two tomato and turkey grilled cheese sandwiches. He soon begins counting the metal keys of different shapes and sizes and estimates there are at least three dozen keys on the ring. He places their sandwiches on the kitchen counter and chuckles as Katarina tries the first key. "You know… skeleton keys are tricky. Sometimes you have to jerk them around to get them to work. The actual key may not even be on that ring."

"It has to be," Katarina says in a spirited voice. "Nana used to say that every door has a key. Every puzzle has a solution. There has to be a key to this box."

"I'm sure there is, but that can wait. You have to eat."

Katarina runs to the counter, takes three large bites of her sandwich and then returns to her task. With her mouth full, she asks, "Can I have chips too?"

"Sure. But then we have to go to sleep. Tomorrow's a long day."

After another ten minutes, she finishes the sandwich and chips and a second glass of milk. Katarina tries seven keys with no luck. Her thumb and index fingers are sore from twisting the metal with brute little-girl force.

Logan turns off all the lights in the house and urges Katarina to go to bed.

"Fine." Katarina slams the ring of keys down on the countertop and crams the *Book of Whispers* under her arm. "I'll figure this out tomorrow." As she darts up to her room, Jinx runs up the stairs behind her. Slipping on rainbow pajamas, she tucks herself in under pink, white, and purple patchwork covers. At the foot of her bed, Jinx snuggles himself into a ball on top of her blanket.

When Logan reaches her doorframe, Katarina asks, "Do you think Nana was crazy like Mom and Dad say?"

"Crazy? No. She was definitely eccentric... quirky... unusual."

Katarina nods. "Do you believe her stories, the ones about the witches?"

"I always thought the stories were wild and that Nana just had a creative imagination, but I never believed them."

"But she said they were true."

Logan sits down at Katarina's bedside. "Sometimes, Kat, grown-ups tell stories to teach us lessons. I think Nana created those stories to teach you how to be strong and courageous." He thought about telling Katarina about their grandmother's dementia, how the cancerous tumor had probably affected her mind, but he didn't want to extinguish his little sister's impression of her grandmother.

"Do you think I'm crazy for believing in Nana's stories?"

Logan tries hard not to smile, but his cheeks curve upward beneath his eyes.

"Jaz thinks I'm crazy for believing in her stories," Katarina says, looking down to the side of her bed. With a gentle poke of her finger, Katarina pushes her glasses further up the bridge of her nose.

"If believing makes you stronger, wiser, then you'll be better off. If you ask me, it would do Jaz some good to believe in Nana's stories. Now, don't stay up too late reading that book."

"I can't read it, silly. It's written in scribbures, or scribatures."

"Do you mean scriptures?"

"That's what Nana called them. I call them scribbles because that's what they look like to me. I just want to look at the drawings, and then I'll go to sleep."

"Okay. Good night, Kat." He kisses Katarina on the forehead and heads to his room.

Katarina sits for a moment and realizes this is the first time she will look at the *Book of Whispers* without her grandmother. She inhales deeply, closes her eyes, and releases a long breath. "I miss you Nana," she whispers.

Katarina unwinds the leather string from the metal knob and slowly opens the book in her lap to the page where the satin bookmark was left a few days earlier when Agatha last read Katarina a story. At first, Katarina could not look down at the pages in front of her. This is something she did with her grandmother only, never alone or with anyone else, and now it feels wrong even to look at the drawings.

But then, a gentle voice in her mind, her grandmother's voice, says, "It's alright, Kat. I don't mind." Katarina smiles at the sound of her grandmother's words, surely from a memory she can't quite put her finger on. With her eyes closed, Katarina can see her grandmother smiling at her as she did the evening before when she last said goodnight.

Her grandmother's smile and voice cajole Katarina's eyes downward to look at the watercolors that cover the entire left page. A green hillside meadow with white lilies scattered in uneven patterns surrounds a depiction of a woman wearing a long blue dress standing with her arms spread out. Her head is tilted upward toward a yellow sun at the upper left-hand corner of the page. Dragon-like shadows fly across a soft blue sky with only a handful of white clouds.

After lingering on the drawing for a few more seconds, noticing for the first time the detailed texture of the woman's long auburn hair, her eyes float over to the page on the right where the story is written. She gasps. For the very first time in her life, Katarina can read the scribbles.

4

SNAKES

After several gentle nudges, followed by a few firm ones, Kevin fails to wake Katarina from her sleep. His mother's thick, leather-bound book lies open on his daughter's chest as if it were returning Katarina's embrace. He lifts the book to see if that wakes her.

With a slight moan, Katarina opens her eyes. "What time is it?"

"It's nine in the morning. The wake will start soon." Kevin places a piece of paper in the middle of the book to save her place, closes it, and lays it on Katarina's nightstand. "I hope you didn't stay up too late."

She shrugs her shoulders and rubs her eyes. "Daddy, what's a wake for?"

"For Nana's friends and family, so they can say goodbye and see her one last time."

The thumping of Katarina's heart causes her to slightly hyperventilate. Zombies appear in her head alongside dark, skeletal characters like those from the animated movies she's seen. She has never thought of her grandmother being dead like that. She never really thought about death before now. *Will Nana look like a dead body? Will Nana's hands and feet drag with her skin hanging from her bones? Will she be able to speak?*

"Are you alright, Kat?" Kevin asks. He sits at the edge of her bed and strokes her messy hair.

With tears welling up in her eyes, Katarina pleads, "I

don't want to see Nana again. Please, Daddy. Don't make me see Nana dead. I don't want to see her dead." She digs her head into her father's chest and tries hard not to cry.

Kevin sighs. "Okay. Let me talk to your mother. Mrs. Castro is already downstairs cooking a big luncheon for later, for when everyone comes over after the burial. She insisted, and you know how Mrs. Castro is about food."

"'Home-cooked food makes everyone feel better,'" Katarina says in a deep, Mexican-accented voice, mimicking one of Mrs. Castro's favorite sayings. They both smile.

"She's not going to the wake?"

Kevin shakes his head. "I think this is Mrs. Castro's way of saying goodbye, by doing the thing she loves the most for Nana, and for us. I'm sure she won't mind watching over you for a few hours."

Katarina's breathing returns to normal. "Thanks, Dad."

Jasmyn walks into Katarina's room and sees her father sitting on Katarina's bed with his arm around her, holding her close. "Here's your dress. Mom ironed it."

"Kat's not going."

"Why not?"

Kevin leans in close to Jasmyn and whispers, "Because she's suffering."

"We're all suffering, Dad." Jasmyn glares at her father. *When do I get a hug?* She glances at Katarina from the corner of her eye.

Kevin stands tall, glowers down at Jasmyn, and steps in front of her to block her view of Katarina. He whispers harshly, "Just leave her alone and get dressed. Now."

Before Jasmyn could retort, a heavy pressure clamps down on her shoulders, as if invisible arms are pressing down along her clavicle bones. She doesn't wince or whine. She inhales a slow, long, deep breath and holds the air in her lungs, counting the heartbeats echoing in her ears, waiting for the sensation to pass. It ends the instant her father walks downstairs.

After finally releasing the air from her lungs, Jasmyn pushes through the tightness in her throat and swallows.

"Are you okay?" Katarina asks, noticing Jasmyn's eyes fluctuating wildly about the room.

"I'm fine," she replies, and heads to her room convinced she showed no signs of weakness.

While buttoning his white dress shirt over his black trouser pants in his room, Logan spots Jasmyn slamming her bedroom door shut. "What's going on?" he asks Katarina as he stands in her doorway.

"I think Jaz is mad at me again," she says, crawling back under the covers.

Logan sits next to her on her bed. "What a surprise."

"Why does she hate me so much?"

"She doesn't hate you."

"But she looks at me like she hates me."

"Somewhere, deep down inside, is a sister who loves you."

"How deep?"

"You may have to dig to China and back, and maybe you'll find her. But then she might be wearing a red Chinese dragon suit and dancing around with firecrackers blasting all over the place." Katarina giggles and wipes her eyes.

"Then you'll have to defeat her demonic breath with tickles and hugs and kisses," Logan continues as he pokes Katarina through the blanket, making her giggle. "And then maybe, just maybe, you'll find her there."

"No, no," Katarina says excitedly. She climbs out from under her blankets and kneels on her bed with her arms lifted high.

"Then I'll have to cast a truth-telling spell and tell her that if she doesn't tell me she loves me, then I'll turn her to stone!"

"You know, she might choose to turn to stone."

Her arms and shoulders droop. "I know," she says with a half-smile spread across her face. An idea pops into her head and her index finger points straight up at the ceiling. "Maybe I'll turn her into a lizard instead of stone. Then I can keep her as my pet."

"Yeah! Then maybe she'll have a heart."

Both Logan and Katarina chuckle as Katarina pretends to pet an imaginary green lizard sitting in her hand. What they don't know is that Jasmyn is standing right outside Katarina's room listening to every single word. After Jasmyn slammed her bedroom door shut, she immediately returned to Katarina to ask her if she had felt the same pressure on her shoulders, the same odd sensation of invisible arms. But when she heard her brother and sister's gossip, her legs froze in mid-stride and her chest began to ache. She hid along the wall leading up to Katarina's room, allowing her tears to quietly stream down her cheeks, wishing she pull herself away from their conversation.

As her brother and sister's giggles grow in volume, as they try and fail to shush their laughter, tears continue to form in Jasmyn's eyes. She wipes them away and commands herself not to cry, pocketing the betrayal for now, holding it in and using it to harden herself against her brother and sister. It reinforces her belief that her family really doesn't want her there—they've never wanted her as part of the family. And although every word hurts her, Jasmyn stays and listens until nothing more is said.

"So what are you going to do while we're gone?" Logan asks after they finish imagining what kind of animal would suit their sister's character best. They choose a snake after alligator, lion, and black bear were disqualified for not being cold enough.

Katarina's eyes light up. "I forgot to tell you! The

drawings and the paintings in the *Book of Whispers*… I can read it all, Logan! All of it! There's this story about an enchanted box. It might be the box I took from Grandma's room, and another story where—"

Logan hears a burst of commotion on the first floor. "Tell me all about it later, Kat. I have to get ready for the wake."

He buttons his cuffs and rushes to his room with his head down. Katarina grabs the *Book of Whispers* and follows close behind on her toes as she rambles on about how the poems in the book sound like magic spells. Both turn toward the right to Logan's room, without noticing Jasmyn standing on the other side of the doorframe.

Katarina plants herself on Logan's unmade bed, pushes the dark blue Jersey cotton sheets into a corner, and opens the *Book of Whispers* in her lap. "This says, 'Crepte, Sconde Dragonde.' And right there is a picture of Gregorn Dragons. Right after that, it says I have to open the box with the key, and the witch who opens the box will have control of the dragons."

"So you are going to spend the day figuring out that little box?" Logan asks as he searches for black dress socks in his sock drawer.

"One of those keys has to be it."

"Sounds like fun, Kat," Logan says as he puts on his shoes.

Fun? Katarina's smile dissipates. "Logan, do you think it's wrong I'm not going to the wake?"

"No. Not at all."

"I mean, I can figure out the box tomorrow. It's just that…"

In the middle of tying his shoelaces, Logan glances up at his little sister who has started combing the end of her frazzled locks with her fingertips. "What is it, Kat?"

"It feels like… Nana left this box for me to find in her room. And she wants me to open it."

He pushes himself up to his feet and sighs. "I heard what you said to Dad. Death is scary."

"I'm scared Nana isn't going to look like Nana when I see her." Katarina's eyebrows wrinkle upwards into sad, pointy arches over her thick glasses.

Having nothing comforting to say, Logan lowers his eyes to the necktie he nervously wraps and unwraps around his fingers.

"Is it bad that I don't say goodbye like everyone else?"

"You have a special way of saying goodbye to Nana, and that's yours and yours alone. Even Dad understands that. You had a bond with Nana none of us had, and if staying home and figuring out this box puzzle is your way of saying goodbye to her, that's fine."

Unsure of her brother's answer, Katarina continues to stare up at him with arched eyebrows. She blinks twice.

Logan smiles. "It's not bad. Trust me."

Katarina nods and takes the *Book of Whispers* back to her room and buries herself under her covers. *I'll figure it out Nana. I'll figure it out for you.*

~ ~ ~

A final brush stroke down Jasmyn's long auburn hair gives her a sense of readiness. She looks at her reflection in the full-length mirror hanging on her closet door. *A cold-hearted snake… That's what they chose to represent me. Why cold-hearted? Because I keep a straight face and don't show my emotions? Because I don't cry whenever someone hurts me? I'd be crying all the time if that wasn't the case. Because I never let anyone know when I'm suffering or scared? Why would I show*

26

anyone what I feel? They wouldn't care. I'm the one without feelings? And now Logan and Kat are making fun of me behind my back. Aren't they being conniving and deceitful, like two boa constrictors plotting to strangle me?

Jasmyn recalls how, yesterday morning, she overheard her parents comfort Katarina through her bedroom wall. She waited for them to knock on her door, to ask if she wanted to "talk about it" or cry in their arms. She waited all afternoon, but the knock never came. Then, in the evening when she went down to get something to eat, she remembered how Logan and Katarina spent the afternoon in their grandmother's room going through her things. No one looked in on her. No one included her. No one consoled her. *Was I always a snake, or did I become one?*

The door to her bedroom slowly squeaks open and her heart flutters. Maybe she was wrong to think poorly of her family. Maybe she's just behaving erratically, having resentful thoughts because she's emotional at her grandmother's death. Maybe her parents will now, finally, ask her if she needs a hug. She watches the door eagerly.

"It's time to go." Her father sticks his head inside but keeps his body in the hallway. "And I don't want you to bug Kat today. Do you hear me? No drama today. Got it?"

The same pressure on her shoulders reappears. Confused and hurt, Jasmyn simply nods without evidence of emotion on her face. Once Kevin closes the door, she exhales as tears brim over her eyelids. Jasmyn brushes the palms of her hands across both her cheeks, wiping them dry, and tries to recall the last time her father said something loving to her, something gentle, caring. She thinks long and hard and comes up with a memory of when she was nine, just before her tenth birthday, just before Katarina was born, when her father said to her, "You'll always be my princess." He hasn't called her princess since. Katarina now holds that title.

They want a snake heart? I'll give them a snake heart!

As Kevin helps Logan put on a necktie in Logan's bedroom, Jasmyn runs downstairs to the kitchen and searches for the small wooden box Katarina described. She finds it, grabs it brusquely, and storms out to the backyard. She places the box on the grass and looks around the yard for something she can use to smash it. *A rake, too inaccurate... a hose, too soft... a lawn chair, too heavy.* Her eyes scan the house wall toward the shed that holds the basketballs and tennis rackets. With determination and hate guiding her stride, Jasmyn throws open the shed door and finds an aluminum baseball bat leaning against the wall.

A wicked smirk crosses her lips. She takes the bat and walks over to the box waiting in the middle of the grass. "Here's your stone cold heart," she whispers as she lines up the bat vertically with the box. Taking a moment to center her alignment, she inhales through her nose and slams the tip of the bat down onto the box's top.

The shattered wooden pieces sprawl out on the grass, fueling Jasmyn's emotional tornado. With her bottom lip trembling with resentment, she drops to her hands and knees and sobs, cursing her brother and sister for excluding her, for teaming up against her, and for bringing her to such an extreme. She lets the high winds blow, round and round, until her tears stop flowing and her breathing normalizes. She has destroyed Katarina's box. There is no turning back.

As remorse begins to settle in, as the whirlwind in her heart dies down to a gentle breeze, the ground below her feet trembles, and an earthquake rips through California.

5

REBIRTH

Three black oval objects stream across the California sky moments after a 6.0 earthquake traverses the west coast. One of the egg-shaped entities burns through thick woods along the mountainside close to the Northern California seashore and is cradled by the surrounding dirt and rock as if the mountain was expecting it and caught it as planned. The second object lands in a dense forest in the southern half of California, also cushioned by a thicket of trees. The third finds its way to a forest at the Nevada border and gently wedges itself into a field of boulders. All three land equidistant from each other and from the source that called them. Before long, the metallic eggs begin to crack. The shells, jagged and dented from traveling through time and space for over three hundred years, crumble once the dragons inside stretch their limbs outward.

The oldest dragon, Oxerion, uncurls the weak muscles in his tail and overextends his back to raise his head to a height of six feet. He flexes his front and hind legs to awaken stiff tendons and cartilage in his limbs, to ignite the rapid blood flow that will make him stronger. At first, he groans at the crackling bones and straining muscles, but then he inhales a lungful of fresh forest air and blows it out slowly, thankfully, acknowledging every bit of oxygen flowing through his nostrils. He sighs once more before taking his first wobbly step.

Once Oxerion steps out of the metallic rubble and onto the fertile land, several hundred one-foot-tall humanoid creatures, with arms and legs almost as thick as their torsos, spill out from the base of the oval casing. They stretch their disproportionate limbs, feeling rejuvenated at the sight of blue skies, green pastures, and ocean water bordering the horizon. Oxerion's minions look up to their master dragon for instructions, their bellies growling with hunger that begs for the nutrients they need to grow to their normal bear-like size.

After several minutes of studying his surroundings and examining his body, Oxerion realizes he doesn't feel subject to Agatha's whim as he did when she entrapped him in his prison chamber. He lifts his shoulders, stomps the ground, and releases the loudest roar his six-foot frame will allow. Weakened from centuries of silence, his throat can only muster a blast with about as much force as the growl of a young black bear. Despite his frustration at his weak roar, which will grow louder with each passing hour, he feels invigorated with freedom. No one commands his actions. There is no witch in control.

Three white seagulls fly across the sky in V formation, squawking as they dart out toward the ocean, reminding Oxerion of his two younger brothers. He closes his large reptilian eyes and focuses on the mental connection between his sibling dragons, the internal link that allows them to communicate with each other telepathically across thousands of miles. He sees Pterones stretching his long limbs on a green hillside without a threat in sight, and Baronyx standing tall on a mountain next to leafy trees, his tar-skinned minions at his side. In monstrous, gargling noises only the Gregorn Dragons can understand, Oxerion shouts, "Pterones! Baronyx! My brothers! It is only a matter of time before we are back to our original form. We must gather and plan our next steps."

Suddenly, the vision of a little girl with glasses appears in Oxerion's mind. He studies her for a moment, watching her giggle without a care in the world. "She is Agatha's kin. I can feel it," Oxerion says to his siblings in what would sound like descending gnarls to the human ear. A rumble emanates from his stomach; Oxerion spots a herd of wild, black-tailed deer and orders his minions to fetch him his meal.

"Are you certain?" Pterones asks.

"I can sense her presence, our bond with her, the same way we were connected to Agatha."

"We are not under her command!" Pterones yelps as he senses the lack of governing force. "Agatha's kin has freed us. Let us rejoice!" He grabs two field rabbits by the legs and tosses them into his mouth.

"This child has Agatha's blood," Oxerion says, chewing on a deer limb. "Although she has freed us, she holds the power to entrap us. We must kill her at once."

Baronyx shakes his head with disappointment. He stretches his red, scaly arms and tail until they unroll to full length as he watches his muscular minions devour a pack of wolves in the corner of an enormous boulder. His stomach grumbles, but it makes him sick to think of killing another living thing, especially a human. Reading his brother's thoughts, Oxerion roars, "You are a sentimental fool, Baronyx. Humans would not hesitate to kill us, and yet you feel sorry for them."

"It is your fault we are at odds with the witches." Baronyx stands tall and faces west toward the source of the bond. "I remember everything."

A freshly peeled rabbit skeleton flies out of Pterones's snout. "You willingly joined our cause, Baronyx. No one forced you to partake."

"Because of Oxerion's lies."

"We are your brothers!" Pterones hisses. "If we cannot depend on each other—"

"Silence!" Oxerion's deep voice echoes in their minds. "We must kill the girl, or she will entrap us again. Do you object to that, Baronyx?"

"She may very well leave us alone. Why look for trouble, Oxerion?"

Oxerion responds with a rough, baritone chuckle. "As we speak, I can feel the pull of her power." He bends his back inward and cracks each vertebra along his spine all the way down to the tip of his sharp tail. "Knowing our history with the witches, do you think Agatha's kin will not hunt us? Do you think she will not imprison us just as Agatha did?"

Both choices are bleak for Baronyx. To kill a human child goes against everything his mother taught him, everything that makes him different from Oxerion. Because his brothers can see and hear his thoughts, Baronyx tries hard to stop thinking of the innocence of the little girl, of the peaceful era with the witches before Oxerion's uprising, of his gentle mother Finna and her daughter Agatha, whom he loved so very much.

Instead, he shifts his mind to remember his years frozen in Agatha's spell with nothing but his brothers' twisted ideas traveling through his mind. He recalls struggling with his own heart, keeping himself from becoming cruel and uncaring, from going insane with rage and thoughts of vengeance. The harsh punishment he and his two brothers endured, trapped for over three centuries in a half-sleep state when they desired to be conscious, pulled awake when all he wished was to leave the world behind, a punishment Baronyx believes is worse than death itself, causes a deep ache in his chest.

"Wasn't Agatha able to read my mind?" Baronyx asks, searching the ground for an answer. "She knew I loved her. She knew I was sorry. We have been asleep, dormant, barely alive for three centuries. Does that not count for anything? Have we not

32

served our sentence and earned our freedom?"

After a short silence, Pterones whispers, "The witches do not care about us. We have to take care of each other, Brother."

"If we don't destroy that witch, she will surely hunt us down and entrap us again," Oxerion says. "I will not wait to be taken back to prison. We must destroy her."

"Baronyx, you know Oxerion speaks the truth. Will you help us kill her so we may survive? Are you with us, Brother?"

With a tone matching his defeated posture, Baronyx nods, "I am with you."

Both Pterones and Oxerion roar to the clear blue sky while Baronyx leans against a massive boulder, contemplating the change in circumstances. Would he decide differently if the witches had listened to his pleas for forgiveness? Would he still follow Oxerion and Pterones if there were others dragons to consider? What other choice is there? To be alone? That is not an option. They have a better chance of survival sticking together, even better if they kill the child witch.

"You have chosen wisely, Brother," Oxerion says. "We are stronger if we stay together, if we fight for one another."

"Do not try to console me, Oxerion. This is the less revolting choice of the few that I have. Besides, I cannot abandon Pterones. He is the youngest. He needs us both."

Knowing Baronyx favors Pterones over him, Oxerion is content accepting whatever loyalty Baronyx is willing to give.

Taking his first steps down the mountainside of the Toiyabe National Forest in Nevada gives Baronyx little pleasure as he begins his journey toward their so-called freedom. At his landing site in Los Padres National Forest in Southern California, Pterones clumsily stomps through thick, leafy bushes like a toddler walking through a stack of toys, knocking down every object in his way. Oxerion commands his minions to follow him away from the seashore in Mendocino National Forest in Northern California to walk southwards along the shoreline. The three Gregorn Dragons slowly begin their daylong march to Katarina's home in San Francisco.

6

AFTERSHOCK

As the tremors roll to a stop, Paula and Kevin huddle with their three children in the backyard. Mrs. Castro kneels by a lawn chair, still holding a wooden cooking spoon. They wait three, five, eight minutes, and then all of them sit down on the ground, breathing half-steadily, looking around the backyard as if they expect something to jump over their six-foot white fence. Birds begin chirping high above in their orange tree, and a few car alarms blare in the distance. After several minutes, they rise to enter the house.

Jasmyn feels uneasy, her stomach twisting and gurgling. She runs to the bathroom at the end of the kitchen and pukes into the toilet bowl. Paula runs in after her and holds Jasmyn's hair up as she vomits. After heaving, crying, and regurgitating once more, she finally washes her face and sits on the toilet seat.

"Don't move," Paula says as she kneels down in front of Jasmyn and wipes her forehead with a damp cloth. "What did you eat last night?"

"A turkey sandwich. But… I… I feel…"

Jasmyn gets lost in a trance, in blurry visions that slowly sharpen before her eyes. Enormous dragons fly high above jagged mountains and crystal blue shorelines, cutting across the sky as easily and smoothly as the ocean's wind. She sees an animal with a lion's body, an eagle's head, and feathery wings standing at the edge of a cliff. For a few moments it soars through a stretch of clouds before a black dragon snaps its jaws into its midsection.

"Jaz?" Paula presses the back of her hand against her daughter's forehead and cheeks.

A woman with wavy auburn hair stands on another cliff, her long brown skirt and white blouse flapping against strong gusts of air. She raises her hands above her head, with the tips of her fingers pointing outward, and aims them toward two large brown dragons in the sky.

"Kevin! Come quick. Something's wrong with Jaz!"

Rays of light shoot from the woman's hands and hit the dragons just as they release sprays of fire from their snouts. They roar with pain and slam into the mountainside, causing a deafening crackle of ancient rock breaking open. The woman's hands stay steady, with the lightning still beaming against the dragons' chests and necks. She speaks words in a language Jasmyn doesn't comprehend, and the dragons burst into ashes.

The woman slowly turns around, eyes closed, allowing the breeze to caress her face, reveling in the silence she has created. Then she opens her eyes to meet Jasmyn's stare.

"What is it Jaz?" Paula shouts. "What's wrong? Talk to me!"

"Do you know who I am?" the woman asks, without moving her lips.

"No."

"No? No to what?" Paula snaps her fingers in front of Jasmyn's eyes. "Talk to me, Jaz!"

"Yes, you do." The corners of the woman's lips shift slightly upward and her eyebrows arch sadly. "I am Agatha. This is who you are."

Jasmyn shakes her head.

"Jaz? Do you see something?" Paula cradles her daughter's face in her hands. "Tell me what you see."

Staring past the bathroom wall tile she stretches a hand

36

forward and whispers, "Nana..."

"Jaz, look at me!" Paula shakes Jasmyn by her shoulders and out of her trance. Jasmyn blinks wildly before turning to her mother. "There. Focus on me, okay? Just sit there and breathe."

"My head hurts," Jasmyn mumbles as she leans her head against the bathroom wall.

With the house phone in his hand, Kevin asks, "Did you hit your head?" He probes his daughter's scalp searching for bumps. "Maybe we should call the paramedics."

"I didn't hit my head. I'm fine. I'm just... tired. I didn't get much sleep last night."

"Just stay here and rest." After assigning Logan and Katarina the task of monitoring Jasmyn resting in the bathroom, Paula pulls Kevin toward the patio door. "She was hallucinating about your mother. She said she saw Nana. She reached out her arm as if she was trying to touch something."

Kevin rubs his eyes with his fingertips. "She's just tired. I doubt any of us slept well these last two nights."

"She was staring right through the bathroom wall as if she was looking at something far away."

With a not-so-subtle jerk of his head, Kevin peeks over at Jasmyn, who now looks annoyed at being told to stay in the bathroom by her younger brother. They watch her closely as she walks toward the kitchen table, Logan holding her elbow like a nurse would hold an elderly woman unable to walk. Paula pulls out a chair and sits facing her daughter at the other side of the table. From the counter, with his arms tightly crossed, Kevin studies Jasmyn's slow motions from head to toe. Logan, who now stands behind his mother, gawks at his sister, his forehead wrinkled.

Jasmyn meets everyone's eyes one by one. *They're going to think I'm nuts if I tell them what I just saw. What the hell did I see anyway? She looked like me, wearing a peasant dress, standing on a mountain, killing those dragons. Maybe I'm going crazy. Could it have been Nana talking to me? No. That's ridiculous. I'm just tired.* She sits up tall and shrugs her shoulders as if nothing had happened. "What's everyone looking at?"

A tsk and a quick wave of Logan's hand dismisses her question. "She's fine."

"Are you alright?" Paula asks.

"I'm fine, Mom, really. I think I just had a dizzy spell. I'll be fine."

Paula sits back in her chair and sighs. "Alright, I'll call the funeral home and see if the wake is still happening. Kevin, can you check the news and see how bad it is out there?"

After Katarina finishes the bottle of lavender air freshener spray, she closes the bathroom door and walks into the kitchen, coughing from the mist invading her lungs. When she reaches the kitchen table, Katarina shrieks. "Hey! Where's my box?"

"What box?" Logan asks.

"The box we got from Nana's room last night—it was part of the dragon spell!"

"Oh, here we go again," Jasmyn mumbles while rolling her eyes. "There are more important things than your little magic toys."

"But the spell…" Katarina says, her breath quickening. "Whoever opens the box…"

"I smashed the stupid box, okay!" Jasmyn yells while rubbing her temples with her fingertips.

As her bottom lip begins to quiver, Katarina takes two steps backwards before running out of the kitchen in tears.

"What's the matter with you?" Logan clenches his teeth. "Why?"

"What? It was just a stupid box sitting on the counter.

How was I supposed to know she would freak out if—"

"But why would you just destroy it? You knew Kat wanted to open it, didn't you?"

Jasmyn's face turns beet red. She stands, staring at the ground with nothing to say, then slowly meets her brother's eyes. "Maybe if you and Kat hadn't split all of Nana's things without me, and maybe if you didn't give me a cold-blooded snake heart, then just *maybe* I wouldn't have destroyed Kat's box."

Logan's lips part, and he can't find words to defend himself from her accusations. His stomach aches with humiliation. Dodging her stare, unable to form an apology, much less swallow the boulder that has formed in his throat, Logan steps backwards away from Jasmyn.

"I heard everything," Jasmyn whispers through a sob she quickly stifles.

"I'm sorry," Logan says in a low whisper. "We were just..."

When he attempts to look up at Jasmyn and sees her standing there in self-righteous indignation, Logan's sad eyes narrow at the realization that Jasmyn's actions were calculated and purposeful and had only one goal: to cause Katarina pain. "You knew destroying Nana's box would hurt Kat."

"Oh...my...God! Is everything *always* about Kat? The entire universe doesn't revolve around her!"

"We weren't trying to hurt you! I'm sorry you heard us laughing about you, but I was trying to make Kat feel better because you were mad at her, again, about who knows what. But you...you..."

Now Jasmyn lowers her eyes to the side, crossing her arms tightly against her chest.

"Kat would never do anything like this to you." A dark realization dawns on Logan, and he shakes his head from side to side, his lips in an angry twist. "You're a heartless bitch," he says flatly, as if stating a fact, not an opinion.

Jasmyn steps back, not because she's shocked by the venom in her brother's words, but because she feels a sharp pressure against her shoulders, the same sensation she had felt when her father scolded her earlier. *What is this?* Her breathing gets heavier, but she maintains a steadiness. *Where is this coming from?* She pushes against the sensations and holds her ground. With her lips pressed into a straight line, she scans the kitchen for some sort of explanation and then returns Logan's glare.

"That's enough!" Kevin steps into the kitchen and between the two siblings. "The funeral is still on. Jaz, go outside and wait in the car."

Keeping her breathing under control while straightening her back against the weight of the force, Jasmyn walks out of the kitchen and heads outside without looking at her father or brother.

Once the front door shuts behind his sister, Logan turns to his father. "You know, I understand when you guys give Kat all the attention and Jaz retaliates, but this? She wanted to get even with Kat. She didn't direct any of her retaliation at me, just Kat. She's only eight, and she just lost her grandmother, and she knows her sister hates her, and..." Logan passes his fingers through his hair and releases a long exhale. "Jaz makes it really hard to not take sides, you know? I understand why she's mad at you guys, but it's not Kat's fault you give her so much attention. She shouldn't take it out on her."

An unfamiliar wrinkle appears above Kevin's eyebrows. "Does Jaz often retaliate because of the attention we give Kat?"

Logan shrugs his shoulders. "You do give Kat the most attention. Sometimes it feels like you ignore us. But... she's a kid. She used to be sick. I get it. I just wish Jaz would get it too."

The words take a second to sink in, but Kevin eventually

understands and swallows hard as he realizes the similarity of his son's actions. "And now... you and Kat split Nana's things without her."

"Does that really matter? We didn't mean to exclude her."

"I never meant to ignore you two either."

The family photo of the five of them that hangs in the living room, taken shortly after Katarina was born, catches Kevin's attention. Everyone is dressed up in black, white, and red, including Baby Katarina. Nothing but smiles and happy faces shine through the photo. It now hangs at an odd angle on the wall behind the couch, tilted by the earthquake. Kevin reaches over the couch to straighten the frame. He looks around the living room and rearranges a few more displaced objects as he speaks.

"When Jaz was younger, she and Nana were close. You know how she read to Kat from that old book? Well, she used to read that book to Jaz when she was younger. When Kat was born, because of her condition, Nana started spending less time with Jaz. We all kind of focused on Kat." Kevin swallows hard as the memories of a sickly, underweight, premature Katarina flash through his mind. It wasn't until Katarina was five that her heart condition "miraculously" disappeared, and Kevin and Paula were able to breath normally again.

Logan crosses his arms and frowns, remembering how he felt neglected during those first few years of Katarina's childhood. A shiver runs down his spine as he recalls Katarina's arms hooked up to tubes in a hospital bed awaiting a procedure. He hated going to the hospital, and seeing his baby sister so helpless.

After fixing the pile of magazines on the coffee table, Kevin runs both his hands through his hair and then rubs his face. He walks to the kitchen to grab his suit jacket and returns. "When Nana learned Kat was sick, she got into herbal and holistic treatment and started performing these weird ceremonies in her room. She would sit for hours in the library studying and researching. She spent less and less time with Jaz and more time with Kat performing all these rituals." Kevin stuffs his hands in his pockets. "The cancer really did a number on Nana once it spread to her brain. I heard her whisper to Kat, when she was still a baby, that she was going to cure her with magic."

"But she's fine now, right?"

Kevin nods. "It just disappeared when she turned five. The doctors didn't know what to make of it."

"I know, Dad, but..." Logan walks around the coffee table and sits in the armchair. "You still act as though something is wrong with her. You and Mom focus on her so much that..." He shakes his head. "I can see that it bothers Jaz, especially because Kat's not sick anymore." Logan scans the ceiling in search of the exact words he wants to say. "I guess I'm saying that when Kat got better, and we knew she was going to be fine, we just thought you and Mom would pay us a little more attention. That's all." He shrugs his shoulders dismissively.

Sitting down on the couch and leaning his arms on his knees, Kevin sighs. "I know it's hard for you and Jaz to understand, but there is no other feeling worse than losing your own child." Kevin's voice catches and he clears his throat. "Just thinking about how close we were to losing Kat makes me sick. It left a scar on your mother and me, and... I guess... it's taking a long time for us to get over it."

Logan nods and watches his father as he sits on the couch staring at his hands, shaking his head as if trying to erase a thought from his mind. He stands with his suit jacket in his hand. Logan stands with him, looks out the window to the car, and turns back to his father. "Maybe you should tell that to Jaz. If she knew that you and Mom are still getting over it, then maybe she'll act differently."

"Maybe." Kevin slips on his suit jacket. "Let's just get through the day. We'll talk more about this later."

As Logan watches his father fix his tie in the dining room mirror, he suddenly sees a man many years older than the man he remembers just ten minutes ago. Weathered hands tighten the knot in place as sad eyes look back at him in the glass.

"I'm going to talk to Kat before we go." Before Kevin can object, Logan flies up to the second floor. When he hears his little sister sniffling in her room, he slows down. A thud echoes across the second floor as he slams his foot down on the ground, snapping Katarina to attention. The monstrous roar and banging along the wall leading to her bedroom makes her back stiffen.

"Where's my little sister? I'm so hungry for little sister meat. ROOOOAAAAR!" She uses the corner of her pajama sleeve to dry her swollen eyes. Logan stomps just outside of Katarina's door and makes an exaggerated sniffing noise. "I smell me some delicious little sister meat. ROOOOOAAAAARRRR!"

A smile sneaks through Katarina's sorrow, and she throws her blankets over her head to pretend to hide from the sister-eating monster. She lies still as a rock as the monster sniffs around her room, apparently unaware of her presence under the covers. The monster sniffs and pounds on her white dresser. It sniffs and pounds on her white desk. It sniffs and pounds along her pink- and white-striped wall just above her bed. Katarina covers her mouth to stifle her giggles.

Then, after a few quiet seconds, Katarina's bed jerks left and right at the hands of the sister-eating monster. The monster grabs Katarina's head, and she screams in pure delight.

"This meat looks delicious. ROOOOAAAAR!"

His index fingers deliver gentle pokes, tickling his sister into the usual fits of laughter. After a few seconds he stops his play, and her rosy cheeks and buck teeth smile back. Her bright, honest eyes aren't enough to shake off the unwelcome vision of a life without her. The mind is expert at making one dwell on the unthinkable.

He gives Katarina the strongest hug he has ever given anyone. "I...can't...breathe," Katarina mumbles.

"Feel better?" he asks once he lets her go.

As the intermission ends, and she is reminded of everything that's happened, Katarina lowers her eyes and snuggles back under the covers, burying her head in her pillow. Logan tucks her in tight, kisses her on the back of her head, and tiptoes out of her bedroom.

7

A SINGLE TOUCH

When Patricia finally arrives at the funeral parlor in San Francisco, she feels an inward tug in her chest. Agatha's body lies in a mahogany coffin trimmed with golden handlebars. White daisies and calla lilies fill the room with a moist, bitter scent. A grim-looking man in a brown suit gestures with his arm for Patricia to take a step toward the coffin as if giving her permission. "Please," he says with his hand guiding the path. There are only two other people in the room sitting in different rows toward the rear.

"Where's the family?" Patricia asks in a whisper.

"They're not here yet. There have been a few traffic delays with the tremors."

Patricia huffs. *They call them 'tremors.'*

"They should be here soon. But you can go inside and say goodbye."

Those words weigh heavier on Patricia's heart than the man can begin to imagine. Her initial objective when she left for the airport last night was to come to San Francisco to Agatha's funeral to find the new witch that would join her coven. The thought of saying goodbye to the woman who had risked so much to save so many, the witch who has known Patricia for most of her four-century existence, has eluded her attention until this very moment.

As Patricia inches her way toward the coffin, the image of her own mother appears in her mind. When her mother's hair grayed and her skin wrinkled, her health also diminished. Her aging lungs couldn't handle the crisp northern air. After suffering numerous bouts of coughs and chest infections, she died quietly in her sleep. Even with all her powers, Patricia is no match for Mother Nature.

Several years later she witnessed her younger sister pass at sixty, an old age then, leaving behind two grown men with families of their own. Her nephews and their children are all dead as well. She stopped following her family lineage after her grandnephews passed. Immortality is a double-edged sword that never seems to stop cutting.

Patricia closes her eyes as dozens of other memories twirl inside her head. Patricia, Agatha, and Jezebel were the only survivors of the final battle with the Gregorn Dragons in the seventeenth century. They were the last of their generation, the only ones with knowledge of their history, the last witches penning the final stories in the *Book of Whispers*. Their coven and their history together had bonded them like no family blood ever could. When Jezebel died, less than two centuries ago, Patricia felt the stinging loss of a true sister, a comrade-in-arms. It was the kind of loss that made her question the reason for her existence. Now, with Agatha gone, Patricia is once again reminded of how trivial life is, even the life of a once-immortal witch, and she is nothing more than a speck sitting upon a rock orbiting a random star traveling across an immeasurable universe.

This loneliness often draws Patricia back to the time when she still lived on the Isle of Enid, littered with rustic houses snugged in the foothills of the green mountains. She and her sister witches stand at the top of a summit, overlooking the glittering sea, staring at Mother Nature's vast glory and wonder. That was the most tranquil time in Patricia's long life.

For centuries, Finna's coven protected the natives of the

island from foreign aggressors. Almost every family on the Isle of Enid had a sorceress in the coven, until the war with the dragons reduced the coven to only three witches. As decades passed and the world grew smaller, the stories of witchcraft on the Isle of Enid spread beyond the Northern Sea. Ship after ship arrived filled with men hungry for power. Soon these invasions became too much for three witches to handle.

Patricia's peaceful reminiscence fades as she remembers how she was forced to hide in the mountains once rumors of the witches' everlasting youth were considered proofs of devil worship and black magic. Foreigners were a superstitious lot, and Agatha would constantly remind her sister witches that they were just uneducated and under the rule of people who didn't understand. Ignorance was forgivable in those days, to a degree. Eventually, the three of them were forced to flee the island.

We were so young back then. We forgave everyone. We should have stood up and fought them off. We went through so much together. Who am I left to relate to now?

Though Jezebel's chosen daughter, Regina, is technically part of her coven, Patricia doesn't feel the strong affinity with her that she did with Agatha and Jezebel. Regina wasn't with her in the fight with the dragons. She didn't watch her sister witches turn to ashes or scream in agony as the dragons tore them to pieces. *Regina doesn't know what it's like to lose sister witches in battle. She knows nothing of the guilt of surviving a war or the pain of real loss. She is still a child in our world.*

With a deep breath, Patricia places her hand along the coffin's gold-trimmed rim. Her eyes concentrate on its satin lining as she prepares herself for what she is about to see. When her eyes arrive at Agatha's face, tears form in her eyes—she barely recognizes her. The long, silver, stringy hair flowing over her shoulders and down her chest, the wrinkly ivory-white skin, and the deflated muscles around her cheekbones are all ghastly. Patricia hasn't seen Agatha in decades, and this is how she finds her dear friend. The thought saddens Patricia and creates a boulder of resentment that materializes as a knot in her throat and cramps in her stomach.

Before, Patricia was nervous about looking at Agatha so old and withered; now, she can't stop staring. Her fingers tremble when she reaches for Agatha's hands. When their skin touches, Patricia shudders at the cold and rubbery feel under her fingertips, wishing her own warmth would seep through her skin and into Agatha's body. While holding Agatha with her left hand, Patricia raises her right to tap her forehead with her fingertips before pressing her palm flat against her heart. *From sunlight until night, through birth and death, we all feel the sting of life. Sleep sister, for it is your time to rest. We will live for you.* Patricia wipes a tear streaming down the side of her face. *Until we meet again, dearest Agatha.*

After twenty minutes, the room starts to fill up. Most of the guests are seniors, accompanied by nurses and older children. Each guest takes a few moments to say goodbye to Agatha personally, then takes a seat.

Patricia identifies Kevin the instant he steps into the parlor. He walks up to the open coffin, pauses to face Agatha for a few seconds, and sits down at the far end of the first row near the windows. His family follows close behind.

Unexpectedly, Jasmyn turns her head from her seat and darts an accusatory glare at Patricia, causing the hairs on the back of Patricia's neck to stand. Holding her breath, Patricia maintains her stare until Jasmyn turns back to face the front of the room toward her grandmother's coffin. *That was weird.*

Once the doors of the parlor are closed to begin the sermon, Patricia shakes her head at realizing Katarina is not in the room and neither is the connection between witches of the same coven. *Could she have really chosen the eight-year-old child? Did she choose at all? Oh, you foolish woman. If you weren't dead, I'd slap some sense into you.*

Patricia walks toward a man in a sharp black suit who is talking about going to Kevin's house after the burial. Being naturally charismatic, she falls easily into conversation with him. "I don't see Katarina around. Is she sick?" she asks.

"Katarina was pretty upset," the guy says, casually glancing at Patricia's sleek black skirt suit. His eyes are drawn to the white rose pinned to her jacket. "She'll be at the house later. We're all going to Kevin and Paula's house after the burial."

"I guess I'll see her later then."

Patricia notices the skin around his neck turn pink as he digs his hands into his pockets and looks to the side. She peeks into the strong azure aura surrounding him. She sees a blurry vision of Katarina wearing a princess costume and calling him Sir Gus, her Knight in Shining Armor. Another vision appears of him dressed in a fireman suit climbing up a four-story building to save a family from a three-alarm fire. She sees a past failed relationship that left him heartbroken, and several family dinners with Agatha's grandchildren. She watches another vision of him coaching a boys' Little League team and helping Logan with his batting swing. Visions of selfless moments in this man's life throw themselves at Patricia, and she feels caught off guard, as if she had casually opened the front door only to be blasted by a windstorm. The deep sincerity in his aura is so unrealistically pure she becomes mesmerized.

Though he was sure he had spoken clearly, he repeats the question Patricia failed to acknowledge during her daze. "How do you know Kevin and Paula?"

A bit startled, Patricia replies, "Agatha and I were old

friends…I mean…my mother spoke so much about Agatha. I feel like I know her and her family. She spoke so often of her grandchildren." Patricia sucks in a short breath when she catches him staring at her with his caramel eyes and looks away quickly. *Get it together. So what if he's handsome? So what if he's a gentleman? He's probably like all the others. The instant he gets a notion of what I am, he'll run off screaming and call me a devil-worshiper. These noble do-gooders are nothing but followers of archaic beliefs and rules. Their blood freezes toward anything different.*

"I'm Gustavo, Paula's brother," he says, extending his hand.

"Patricia." She takes his hand in hers.

"It's very nice to meet you, Patricia," he says with half a smile.

Gustavo's touch provokes a warm vibe that climbs up the skin on her hand and snuggles the length of her arm like a tight-knit sweater. She releases his hand and looks away, blushing for the first time in centuries.

~ ~ ~

Katarina spends most of the afternoon in her room with Jinx cuddled up at her feet and the *Book of Whispers* on her lap. She reads through more than half the book, memorizing the poetic words of various incantations, stories that seem too incredible to be true. There are spells that will make people tell the truth, even when they are trying to lie. Others can erase specific memories from a person's mind. More spells lighten the mood of a person feeling upset and frustrated—Katarina plans to try these out on Jasmyn. There are so many invocations to learn, so many stories to read, so many pages to peruse that, by the end of the afternoon,

Katarina's overwhelming excitement sends her crashing into a deep, dreamless sleep. She wakes up to the sound of Logan tapping his finger on her doorframe.

"Wake up sleepyhead."

"What time is it?" Katarina stretches as she looks for her new favorite book, which has slipped onto the rug on her floor.

"It's around six. We're cleaning up. I thought you might want something to eat. Mrs. Castro made a macaroni and cheese casserole, just for you."

"Sure. Is Jaz downstairs too?"

Logan nods. "You have every right to be mad at her. What she did was horrible."

"I'm not upset anymore."

"You should be."

"I know, but...I was thinking about it and...maybe we should have asked her to come with us to Nana's room last night."

"That's no excuse to act like a jerk."

"Didn't you say it's not her fault alone?"

"Yes, but—"

"And didn't you say that she reacts to the way Mom and Dad treat her? So maybe she was hurt because we did stuff without her when we should have included her."

"You can't excuse bad behavior."

"I'm not excusing her. I'm just trying to figure out why she acted that way. Because...she's my sister...and...she loves me, right? I mean, she has to love me, even if it *is* deep down in China. Sisters love each other, right?"

Logan smiles tenderly. "Of course she loves you. And maybe you're right about last night. We should have included her." Logan again wonders if Mom and Dad comforted Jasmyn yesterday. If his parents were too busy to do so, Jasmyn might be even more vulnerable. "I'll talk to Jaz later, try to make up for

51

yesterday. Now, why don't you wash up and come downstairs?"

Katarina feels refreshed after washing her face and putting on the black cotton t-shirt dress her mother ironed for her. The afternoon sun sends a soft glow through her room that reflects off the princess-themed mirror. She combs her auburn wavy hair into a soft ponytail, puts on her glasses, and assesses her outfit in the mirror. *You would have liked this dress, Nana.*

Jinx meets Katarina at the bottom of the steps and barks the instant she arrives at the first-floor landing. She lifts her head to scan the room for Nana's friends from the senior community center and lets out a sigh at finding none. *Good...just family.* After another quick glance, she narrows her eyes at the woman sitting next to her uncle.

~ ~ ~

For a good portion of the afternoon, Patricia and Gustavo stick together like opposing magnets. Patricia spoke about her work and her studies and answered more questions than she normally would have to anyone, and Gustavo did the same.

Both Kevin and Paula noticed Gustavo's attention toward this stranger. When Patricia finally introduced herself to Kevin and Paula, they thought her claim that she knew Agatha through her mother's stories was somewhat odd. But their suspicions were set aside by Gustavo's evident attachment to her. Kevin convinced Paula that Agatha would have been very happy for Gustavo, considering the circumstances under which he and Patricia met.

Earlier, at the cemetery, when the coffin was lowered down into the plot, Patricia lingered at the head of the burial ground long after Kevin and Paula left to talk to Agatha's friends. Gustavo waited for her just a few steps behind, unbeknownst to Patricia. When she turned around and found him standing there with his hands inside his pockets, she felt his aura reaching for her, calling her, waiting for her to allow it to embrace her once more. *So this is why Agatha and Jezebel gave up immortality,* Patricia thinks. But her logic quickly counters, *I'm just feeling extra sensitive because of Agatha's death, that's all. This will pass.*

A dog's bark across the living room draws Patricia's attention. When she sees Katarina standing at the base of the stairs, she senses the witch's bond and quietly gasps. *Katarina's the one.*

"Is something wrong?" Gustavo asks, noticing the change in Patricia's demeanor.

Patricia shakes her head and lifts a glass of water to her lips. "Katarina is exactly as Agatha described." She takes a long sip.

Gustavo looks at Katarina and waves her over. Katarina waves back and holds onto the flaps of her dress while she walks to her uncle. "Kat, this is my friend Patricia. Patricia, this is Princess Katarina of the McKeery Clan."

Katarina smiles at Gustavo's forced Irish accent before looking solemn again.

"Kat was very close to her grandmother," Gustavo says as Patricia empties her glass of water. Gustavo takes the glass to get a refill, leaving Katarina alone with Patricia.

"I bet you two were the best of friends," she says with a mischievous smile.

Katarina nods shyly.

Patricia leans in and whispers, "Do you know about me or Regina?"

Katarina furrows her eyebrows and shakes her head. "Who is Regina?" She reaches for a bowl of raspberries and pops a few into her mouth. "Do you want some?"

With a confused look on her face, Patricia nods. *Katarina has the aura. I sense her presence as a supernatural being. Agatha definitely chose her. Why doesn't she recognize me? Why doesn't she know about Regina?*

Katarina scoops up a few berries to roll into Patricia's palm. Their skin grazes as Patricia cups Katarina's offering. Instead of smoothly rolling the berries into her hand, Katarina's hand opens limply, sending several berries tumbling to the floor. An electrifying energy jolts through Patricia and Katarina as the sacred touch connecting them as sister witches solidifies in their bodies.

This is the same sensation Patricia felt over three centuries ago when her mother performed the Blood Rites Ritual when she was nineteen. Patricia's mother recited a spell over an open fire and transferred her magic with a single ceremonial touch. She saw her mother's memories; she felt her mother's joy and pain, her most secret fears, just as she now sees Katarina's. But that was her mother, a kinswoman, and Patricia was explicitly chosen above her two younger sisters to be her mother's inheritor, as was the tradition. This is how magic is transferred between a sorceress and her successor, or so Patricia thought. *How is this happening? Katarina's not my kin!*

Four hundred years of Patricia's life flow into Katarina's mind. She sees her grandmother, young, standing next to Patricia and other women along a green mountainside, wearing long dresses that flap against the ocean's gusty wind. Images of fantastical creatures, women conducting sorcery and traveling across distant lands become a part of Katarina's memory. She sees war-torn European cities, African tribal lands, South American indigenous women, and other worldly visions spanning decades and centuries.

One memory shows Patricia crying at a small burial ground at the top of a hill by a thick-trunk willow tree. There are twelve mounds of dirt and twelve short headstones, some more weathered than others. Agatha stands beside Patricia, holding her as she sobs. Patricia kisses each headstone and both women walk away. Katarina knows that this was the last of Patricia's family. Another vision shows Regina's induction ceremony, with Agatha and Patricia standing by Jezebel's side as Jezebel performs the Blood Rites Ritual and touched Regina's cheek with her bare hand. She stands tall, with her head held high and her shoulders back, and performs her first magic spell in front of Agatha and Patricia.

Katarina blinks. *That's Nana! That's Patricia with Nana! They are witches, just like in the* Book of Whispers*!*

One after another, like a film-camera reel fast-forwarding and reversing through snapshots, Patricia's memories of Agatha and other witches flow through Katarina's consciousness until she reaches the present day. She knows about Regina, Patricia's true identity, who her grandmother really was, and who she herself, now is. Anxiety mixes with amazement as Katarina absorbs it all like a dry sponge dipped into a bucket of water.

Patricia studies the little girl as she stares blankly at the white rose on her suit jacket, beginning to hyperventilate. After scanning the room to make sure no one notices their interaction, Patricia gently grabs Katarina's arms and gives her a back-and-forth shake. "Katarina," she whispers close to her ear, "come back to me." Blinking, Katarina's eyes begin to focus on Patricia's as she falls out of her trance. They look at each other before Katarina's knees weaken and she faints into Patricia's arms.

8

TRIGGERS

Gustavo grabs his medical gear from his truck, checks Katarina's vitals, and wakes her into a half-sleep state. After a bit of manipulation from a subtle Patricia, Gustavo diagnoses a simple fainting spell and brings Katarina up to her room to rest.

Having witnessed everything without saying a word, Jasmyn follows Gustavo and glues herself to a chair to monitor her sister's recovery. Something about that woman bugs her, and after seeing her touch Katarina just before her faint, Jasmyn distrusts her even more.

The princess-themed bedroom makes Jasmyn nostalgic. She hasn't sat in this room since Katarina was born, since her parents moved her to her current room at the end of the hallway. Maybe it's the pastel curtains with their ends piled up on the floor or the abundance of punch-colored pillows and throw blankets scattered across the area rug; something about this bedroom seems smaller than she remembers. A low groan escapes her when she raises her feet onto the fuzzy top of Katarina's ottoman. The alarm clock on the nightstand slowly ticks away as she waits for her sister to wake up.

As she studies her sister's breathing, Jasmyn feels a pull toward her, like a magnet attracting every inch of her body to Katarina. It reminds her of the sensation she felt when she walked into the funeral home, when she saw that woman in the back standing next to her Uncle Gustavo. Something about that woman attracted Jasmyn's attention then; something about Katarina draws her now. As with anything out of her control, she pushes back and shakes it off.

Katarina's baby face takes Jasmyn back to the days after her sister was brought home from the hospital. Jasmyn and Logan weren't allowed to touch her or play with her. She was "special," and required extra attention. *Mom and Dad called you Princess Katarina from the very first day.* Her gaze moves toward the floor as she tries to remember the last time her parents called her "princess." It was a long time ago. *No matter. I'll be out of this house and at Berkeley in the fall.* An overdue yawn consumes her. Jasmyn stretches before snuggling under a violet fleece blanket. *You can have Mom and Dad. They'll barely miss me anyway.*

~ ~ ~

A deep blue evening sky covers Florida's western coastline as the stars begin to twinkle in the east. Regina's eyes adjust to the darkness as she rises from her bed for the first time since yesterday morning. She looks out toward the horizon and wonders why she felt so sick; she hasn't been that sick since her mother died. Her mother's death was brutal to the point of nausea, but she was expecting it, her mother had prepared her for it. What could have caused such a physical reaction from her now? Her symptoms yesterday were debilitating, and although she feels better today something still lingers inside of her making her anxious.

Could it be some kind of dark magic? She rushes to her phone and finds it uncharged. She connects the charger and sees several text messages from Patricia.

"It took you long enough," Patricia whispers when she answers her cell phone.

"What's happened?" Regina asks with a cough.

Patricia steps out to the backyard and slides the patio door shut behind her. "Agatha died yesterday."

"Hold on." Regina lowers the phone to her hip, taps her forehead with the fingertips of her right hand and presses her palm against her chest. "From sunlight until night, through birth and death, we all feel the sting of life. Sleep sister, for it is your time to rest. We will live for you." Tears flow down her cheeks. After a minute, Regina chants an Ojibwe prayer in a low voice, grimacing at specific moments in the song. She moves her hand up and down and in a flowing pattern in front of her body, accentuating certain parts of the hymn.

Patricia rolls her eyes as she waits. *Regina and her fetish for Native American guys. She's probably humming a death prayer she learned from Erik. Or was it Ricardo?* She glances at her wristwatch. *I'm giving her one more minute.*

Finally, Regina takes a deep breath and rubs her stomach before lifting the cell phone back to her ear. "That's why I was so sick yesterday."

"Yes. We all suffer when we lose one of our own."

"Were you sick too?"

"Nothing I haven't gone through before."

A single tear sneak down Regina's cheeks as she stares out at the fading orange hue bordering the horizon. As night settles in, she remembers the last time she saw Agatha - it's been decades. She clears her throat. "She had two granddaughters. Did she choose a successor?"

"It seems she chose Katarina, the younger one. She's only eight."

With long, lagging strides, Patricia paces back and forth across the stone patio as she gives Regina a summary of the day. Gustavo smiles at her intermittently through the sliding glass door. She smiles back, inhales deeply, and turns away from his view.

"You inducted her?" Regina shakes her head. "Wait. I don't understand. You performed the Blood Rites Ritual on Katarina?"

"No. *I* didn't *do* anything. It wasn't intentional. I just touched her and I felt the shock—the same shock I felt when my mother inducted me. I saw Katarina's thoughts and memories. It was an induction, I'm sure of it."

"I didn't know anyone but your own family could give you the sacred touch."

"Neither did I. It's never been done, at least, not that I know of. Katarina didn't take it well. She passed out in front of her whole family. She's been asleep for two hours."

Regina opens a glass bottle of water from her refrigerator and takes a swig. "Agatha was a torn woman. When I spoke to her last, about ten years ago, she told me she was sharing our history with her granddaughter, but she didn't want her to be a witch. Passing down her gift goes against everything she ever spoke about. She wanted them to have a normal mortal life. But, do you think…?"

"What?"

"Maybe she changed her mind at the last second?"

"Like on her death bed?"

"And then, maybe, since she couldn't finish the ritual..."

"I finished it for her."

"Seems likely, right?"

Patricia shakes her head. "I wish she had stuck to her plan. Then all I'd have to do is collect her relics and be gone. Instead, I have to explain everything to her family. Me—someone they've never met. They're going to burn me, you know. Seriously. With real fire."

"You'll be fine. You're a charismatic goddess. They'll love you."

"They already hate me." Patricia looks at Paula, Kevin, and Gustavo through the patio doors. "Paula, Agatha's daughter-in-law, senses I had something to do with Katarina's fainting spell."

"Just be open and honest. They'll understand. And don't get offended if they don't. Wait…what am I saying? You're an easy trigger. I bet you a thousand bucks you'll end up freezing them in a sheet of ice."

"I am not an easy trigger. I just don't like it when people attack me. That's all. Everyone gets defensive when they're being attacked."

"Yes, but not everyone has the powers you do."

"Okay, I promise not to be too sensitive. Happy?"

"Yes." Regina's stomach gurgles. Her chest feels tight, as if her shirt is compressing her torso inward. "How long is this going to last? I feel like throwing up again."

"You should be over it by now."

"I still feel…nervous, as if something big is about to happen…something dark. Does that sound weird?"

Patricia scans the purple rose bushes at the base of the white fence, concentrating, searching for the same sensation Regina is feeling. When one witch feels an omen, all witches feel an omen. "Now that you mention it, I do feel something, but…I can't say what it is. I can't look into it right now. Do you think you might be pregnant?"

"What?!"

"I had a similar feeling when Agatha became pregnant. Although…" Patricia cocks her hips to the side and looks up toward the sky. She smirks at the flash of memory. "It may have been a psychedelic reaction to LSD. I was high when Agatha told me the news. I was doing a ton of drugs back then. It was amazing how much LSD I took to get high—it would have killed any

60

mortal."

"I'm not pregnant! And can you stop joking around!"

"When you're three hundred ninety-nine years old, you'll find a little sliver of humor behind every dark cloud."

"You know, I'm nearly half your age."

"I wonder when your sense of humor will kick in."

"Can you please focus? I don't like this feeling."

"Okay. I have Agatha's family to deal with first. I'll look into it afterward. But seriously, are you sure you're not pregnant?"

Regina grunts and hangs up the phone.

~ ~ ~

"She's a photographer for *Vogue*," Gustavo says as Paula grills him about Patricia. "She lives in New York City."

"Oh, so this is some sort of funeral fling?" Paula asks, her eyes darting toward the backyard where Patricia is talking on her phone.

"No." He looks toward the glass doors. Patricia gives him a secretive wave. Gustavo waves back.

Kevin chuckles, but then clears his throat when Paula glares at him. "So what if it is? It's none of our business, Paula."

"It is my business when she makes my daughter pass out."

"You don't know what made Kat faint," Kevin says. "She's been upset. She hasn't had anything to eat all day."

Gustavo nods.

"There's something weird about her. You don't really buy that story about her mother being one of Agatha's friends in the senior center, and about how she feels close to us from hearing stories from Agatha, do you? Who does that?"

Both Gustavo and Kevin shrug their shoulders.

Morons. Paula shakes her head. *A beautiful woman can*

turn the smartest guys into complete idiots.

~ ~ ~

The rose bushes fail to tell Patricia anything. The shading trees and thick grass in the backyard also remain silent. Mother Nature is the universal communicator and usually delivers her warnings through the whispers of the wild. But these plants are all man-derived, on chemically-treated soil. There is nothing natural about this landscape, so Patricia learns nothing of the omen. She will have to work on it later.

When Patricia walks back into the kitchen, Paula doesn't hesitate. "Did you have anything to do with Kat passing out?"

Patricia sees now that Paula isn't going to be easily persuaded. Her intentions are honest and simple—she's protecting her children from potential danger. She remembers the same intense look on Agatha's face when she last saw her at the hospital so many years ago.

"Yes," Patricia says, swallowing hard. "I did."

"What are you saying?" Gustavo rises from his seat.

Patricia's eyes can't break away from Paula's stare. She has to receive the hate beaming from her eyes, to take the brunt of the deception Agatha built up. It's her atonement for leaving when Kevin was born, for abandoning Agatha instead of adapting and staying with her sister witch. She sighs. *They're going to hate me, but it doesn't matter. It's not about me. Not this time.*

With her hands folded, Patricia inhales and looks at Kevin. "Did Agatha ever speak to you about her magic? Did she ever tell you stories about her coven?"

"When I was a kid she told me stories about being part of a witches' coven, about having magic powers, about being immortal, but they were just stories." Kevin says with a chuckle.

62

"What about them?"

"They aren't just stories. Agatha was a powerful sorceress, part of an ancient coven of witches from the Isle of Enid. You all thought she was ninety-three years old, but she was really three hundred sixty-three years old when she died."

Kevin's skin tingles with curiosity. No one has ever backed up his mother's claims of magical powers, validated the stories she claimed were true but seemed too far-fetched to be real.

"The gift of magic can only be passed to a female family member down Agatha's bloodline. She had no daughters, but she did have granddaughters. It seems she decided to give Katarina her gift."

"Are you saying Kat is a witch?" Kevin asks.

Patricia presses her lips together and nods.

Paula shakes her head. "First she makes Kat faint, and now she says that my little girl is a witch. And we're supposed to trust whatever she says? How could you not know if your mother had supernatural powers? She was your own mother, and you didn't know?"

But Kevin did know, he just hadn't realized it until this very moment. Kevin recalls how sad his mother seemed when her offers to read from the ancient book were turned down by an eleven-year-old boy who wanted to hang out with his middle school friends. Any notion of magic spells or witches stories were considered to be the workings of a little boy's imagination, not the budding ideas of big kids in middle school. Young Kevin shoved his mother's stories and magic to the back of his mind, the way a child shoves baby toys to the back of a toy bin, and grew up.

"My mother used to read the book to Jaz when she was younger, and to Kat up until she passed away," Kevin says. "She tried to tell me when I was a kid, but," he shakes his head with exasperation. "Why didn't she just demonstrate her magic to all of us? I was stupid kid back then. Now, I would have believed her."

"When she gave birth to you, Agatha became mortal. She started aging, deteriorating as any person would, and her powers weakened as well. While she was pregnant, she spoke of hiding her magic so you could live a normal life. Elliot was a religious man; that's not a bad thing, but truly devout people have treated us poorly in the past, and she didn't want to lose Elliot or jeopardize the family and the home she had built. Agatha felt she had to keep her powers hidden." Patricia huffs to the side as the irony sinks in. She, of all people, is defending Agatha's choice.

"Then why tell us the stories?" Kevin asks. "Why even mention the *Book of Whispers*?"

"I wish I knew. Maybe with you, Kevin, it didn't seem rational to push it since you could never be her successor. But when you had daughters, Agatha saw a second chance. Maybe she had a change of heart because Elliot had passed away and you were older. But by then, she was older and her powers were weak. She couldn't show you enough to make you believe. So, she shared her stories with the girls so they would know about her magic, remember her for it."

"And what about Kat?" Kevin asks. "My mother actually chose Kat over Jaz to inherit her powers?"

"Katarina has a witch's aura. Jasmyn doesn't. Now I have to talk to Katarina about—"

"No!" Paula interrupts.

"Paula..." Kevin says.

"I don't want her anywhere near my children."

Patricia's tone hardens. "I didn't *want* Katarina to faint. It just happened."

"What did you do to Kat anyway?" Paula asks, narrowing her eyes. "Why *did* she faint? What else is going to 'just happen' while you're here?"

"I am not here to hurt anyone, if that's what you're thinking."

"You have already proven otherwise," Paula says, standing only a few feet in front of Patricia.

"If I wanted to hurt you, I would have already done so, and you would not have seen it coming."

Pointing at the front door, Paula says, "Get out of my house."

"I am not leaving until I have a chance to talk to Katarina."

Paula narrows her eyes, takes one step closer and says in a calmer, more authoritative tone, "I'm going to say this one last time. Get out of my house. Now."

Patricia suspects that, if she objects, Paula will physically attack her. Paula is stubborn, like a lioness that will never give up her cubs to a predator no matter how big the predator is. That, in Patricia's opinion, is understandable, even respectable, but counterproductive at the moment. She is going to have to prove her trustworthiness.

"No." Patricia says, and just as she expects, Paula raises her arms to push Patricia backwards toward the patio door. But before Paula has a chance to move forward, a crystallized sheet flows over her body, freezing her in place. Only her eyeballs retain the ability to move. Both Gustavo and Kevin shout and charge at Patricia, but she holds up her hands and encases them in ice as well.

"Don't!" Patricia shouts at Logan, who stands in the doorway to the living room. "I promise this will end well," she says. He nods nervously and takes a step backwards.

Cursing, Patricia places her hand on the kitchen counter and leans over for a moment. *Damn those elemental spells. I always forget how they drain me. I'm out of practice.* Standing tall against the fresh soreness in her muscles, Patricia recites another spell and now everyone moves freely, as if it had never happened.

Kevin, Paula, and Gustavo stumble around the kitchen before bending over, their hearts beating faster than they ever thought possible. Logan helps his mother to a seat at the table.

Concealing her discomfort with slow, steady breaths, Patricia says, "You would never have seen it coming."

Paula nods, leaning against Kevin as he places his arm around her shoulders. Everyone waits for Patricia to continue her explanation.

"Agatha was a witch, and now Katarina is one too. I need to make sure whoever possesses the gift knows what she can and can't do. It's a monumental responsibility. She could accidentally cause a lot of harm." Patricia walks closer to the table and addresses Paula. "I'm sorry for casting a spell on you, but I need you to believe me. I'm here to help your daughter. I'm not here to hurt anyone."

Then, at the entrance to the kitchen, a soft shuffling sound interrupts the tense silence. In her purple pajamas and pink monster slippers, Katarina crosses the kitchen to her mother, dragging the heels of her slippers with every slow step. After Paula hugs her, Katarina searches the room for Patricia. She meets her worried stare.

"Is it all true?" Katarina asks in a tone too mature for her age.

Patricia sighs and nods.

They share a smirk, a silent understanding, before Katarina nods back.

"Why don't you tell your mother what you saw when I touched you?" Patricia asks in an unusually maternal tone.

She glances at her father, brother, and uncle before turning around to look straight into her mother's eyes. "I saw Nana...she was younger…with Patricia and other women. There were dragons like in the *Book of Whispers*, and…I saw…" With her hand wrapped around her opposite arm at the elbow, Katarina glances between the floor and her mother, unable to articulate the images in her mind. Her eyes float up toward Patricia.

"Do you want me to tell your mom what you saw?"

Katarina nods and sits on her mother's lap as Patricia explains the sacred touch.

9

STABBED

"It's a lovely morning, isn't it?" Strong winds blow the woman's auburn hair away from her face as Jasmyn gazes at the fabric of her blue medieval dress. Strangers don't normally appear in Jasmyn's dreams, let alone dressed in costumes.

"Who are you?"

The wind blows once more as if answering Jasmyn's question. She forgets the woman and returns to staring at the sea's horizon from their spot on the mountain's summit. The air becomes still and the sun's rays caress Jasmyn's face like a mother's warm hands cradling a baby's cheeks. She turns to the woman and sees she is also basking in the sun's heat.

With her eyes closed, the woman says, "I am within you. I am a part of you. I am inside you and Katarina."

Jasmyn gasps as she wakes up in Katarina's bedroom. When she sees Katarina is no longer in her bed, she jumps to her feet and heads to the staircase. Hushed tones emanate from the kitchen. Sitting at the top of the stairs, she listens closely to the conversations below. After much explanation from a voice she doesn't recognize, Jasmyn hears, "Agatha chose Katarina as her successor. She is the newest witch of our coven."

Our coven? Katarina is a witch? That woman, Patricia, is a witch too. Nana was a witch. I felt a sensation from her the night she died. I felt it from Patricia at the funeral home. And now, Katarina has it. What is this feeling?

"What are you doing there?" Logan asks brusquely from

the base of the stairs on the ground floor, looking up at her with a scowl.

She shrugs in response, rubbing her arms to ease the pinching sensation she suddenly feels.

"Come downstairs."

When Jasmyn walks toward the island counter at the center of the room, she delivers the best straight face she can muster. Along with the tiny spikes from Logan, she feels that pull toward Patricia and Katarina. She glances their way before directing her gaze to a stool. An unusual amount of tension stiffens her neck and shoulders when she senses everyone's eyes upon her, studying her every move, waiting to see her explode. The stool screeches when she sits on it, tearing through the silence in the kitchen. With her eyes aimed at the ground and a thick swallow that echoes in the quiet room, she straightens her back and waits for someone to say something.

"What did you hear?" Patricia finally asks, having watched her entrance carefully.

"I heard it all," Jasmyn says with her eyes still averted. "Nana chose Kat to be her successor. Kat is a sorceress, and I'm not. Nana didn't want me to have her magic."

Patricia nods, sensing the raw sentiment under Jasmyn's stone facade. *She could win Vegas tournaments with that poker face.*

The injustice Jasmyn feels stirs up enough righteous courage for her to meet the eyes peering down at her. "Why is everyone staring at me? Did you all think I would be mad? I don't care. Really, I don't."

"Jasmyn," Patricia says as she takes a step forward. "I know what you must be thinking. Although Agatha didn't choose you, you are still a very important part of Katarina's life."

With a huff, a defiant smirk crosses Jasmyn's face. *It's all about Kat, isn't it? It's always all about Kat.*

Patricia takes another step to place her hand on Jasmyn's shoulder, but Jasmyn stands up abruptly. The leg of her chair screeches along the kitchen floor as she backs away from Patricia's touch. "You don't know anything about me." Her glare travels around the kitchen at everyone staring at her. When she lands on Katarina, their eyes lock for an instant before Jasmyn walks out to the backyard.

"Leave her," Logan says to Patricia. "She's got a chip on her shoulder."

Patricia notices Paula and Kevin rolling their eyes. "I wonder why," she says in a sarcastic tone. She marches out to the backyard before anyone can express an adequate response. Patricia closes the patio door behind her before calling out, "Jasmyn, wait!"

Jasmyn spins to face her. "No, *you* wait! You have no idea what I'm thinking. You have no idea what I'm feeling."

"I know what it's like to not feel wanted," Patricia says. "To believe the people you love don't want you around. To have been overlooked and rejected by someone you thought would never give you up." Her voice cracks. She swallows hard and lowers her voice to a whisper. "I know exactly what that feels like."

A single helicopter flies diagonally across the sky above them. When their eyes meet again, Patricia arches her eyebrows and sighs. "I know more than you think."

Scanning Patricia from the top of her perfectly combed black hair to the pointy tips of her black leather pumps, Jasmyn feels the pull stronger than before. When Patricia steps closer, Jasmyn doesn't step back. She tries to frame the sensation as a question, as something that makes logical sense. "What is this…this…vibration I'm getting from you?"

Patricia stops and tilts her head like a confused puppy. "What vibration?"

The thumping of low-flying helicopters draws their attention once more. Once the choppers disappear behind a row of trees, an explosion in the distance provokes long-range shock waves that nearly knock Patricia and Jasmyn off their feet. More helicopters zip over their heads, heading north toward the bay.

"What the hell was that?" Kevin shouts as he runs outside. They look toward the orange glow in the distance. Dark clouds and smoke rise into the twilight sky. Another shock wave.

Patricia's phone rings. "Now is not a good time, Regina."

"Turn on the news, right now!" Regina yells over the phone.

Patricia runs inside and orders Logan to turn on the news in the living room. The local news station shows live coverage at the Golden Gate Bridge. Flames and smoke fill the screen. A reporter in a helicopter reads from a tablet and shouts at the camera. "Three large reptilian creatures, or dragons as some people are calling them, have been spotted in California. One is attempting to cross the San Francisco Bay, another is in Santa Cruz, and a third is nearing Stockton. All three dragons are followed by dozens of oversized, humanoid beasts. The National Guard is responding to the threat, but their weapons seem to have no effect on the creatures. California is in a state of catastrophe and has called upon the armed forces for help. We will keep you updated of further developments…"

"I'll call you back." She hangs up and searches the room for Katarina. She finds her sitting in Kevin's arms as the rest of the family watches the live coverage.

"Katarina," she calls sharply before taking a breath to calm her tone. "Did you recite anything from the *Book of Whispers*? Did you read any of the spells out loud?"

Katarina nods sheepishly.

"Which ones?"

"I read a few. A couple about enchanting boxes and vases, and one about gray dragons. No, wait, it was grown dragon…"

Patricia swallows. "The Gregorn Dragons?"

Katarina's nod confirms Patricia's fear. She curses under her breath and squeezes her hand into a white-knuckled fist. *Damn it Agatha!*

"Was I not supposed to? I didn't know. I…" Katarina buries her head in Kevin's shoulder.

"It's not your fault," Patricia says, softening her tone. "Your grandmother was supposed to warn you, prepare you so that this wouldn't happen, but it seems she passed away before she had the chance." Katarina's wide eyes calm Patricia's growing frustration. Patricia closes her eyes for a breath and relaxes the muscles in her neck. "By touching you, I've shared my history, my memories, and my knowledge of magic with you. My memories of our coven have become your memories, and from them you can see the powers you possess. Please, Katarina, never recite a spell from the *Book of Whispers* unless you know exactly what you are doing. Okay?"

Katarina nods, feeling relieved that Patricia isn't upset at her. Patricia places her palm on Katarina's cheek and sighs as she realizes how incredibly young Katarina is for such a huge responsibility. She still can't understand why Agatha chose her over Jasmyn. A level of skepticism is required to truly understand the depths of sorcery, to grasp its consequences; this is something Jasmyn clearly possesses. A young, innocent child who trusts everyone and everything is too weak.

"Each of us has a unique gift and unique responsibilities. Your grandmother helped us defeat the Gregorn Dragons by entrapping them in a mystical prison. Only she had the ability to conduct entrapment spells, and now only you have that ability. We have to get the *Book of Whispers* and the relic Agatha used to represent their prison. It was a small wooden box with a lock. I believe it had black metal leaves around its edges. Have you seen it?"

"Jasmyn destroyed it," Logan says.

Patricia's voice drops to a whisper, almost a mumble. "That box is sealed with a dark magic. Nothing can break it, except…" Patricia narrows her eyes at Jasmyn, wondering. "Without that relic, we have no control over them."

"I didn't know," Jasmyn says. "I was mad at Kat and…I wanted to…I wasn't thinking. I smashed it to pieces. I'm sorry."

Patricia doesn't acknowledge Jasmyn's apology the way she did Katarina's. Logan, Paula, and Kevin all glare at Jasmyn, unknowingly sending thousands of invisible daggers at her. Jasmyn lowers her eyes and takes a few deliberate breaths to keep the attack from becoming unbearable. After a few seconds, once everyone stops glaring, it fades.

Patricia paces back and forth in the kitchen for a minute before realizing the solution to this problem—a solution no one will like. If the box was intact, if the relic was sound, then Katarina would have full command of the dragons and would be able to send them back to their prison. *Just read the spell and open and close the box. It could have been that simple. But of course not. You better be sweating buckets up there, Agatha!*

She finally stops in front of Kevin and Paula and looks at them sternly. "We need another box to represent their prison. Katarina is going to have to recite the spell to each of the dragons in their presence. She has to look at them, and they have to acknowledge her and hear her voice. She will open and close the box, and the dragons will disappear."

"Are you insane?" Paula says. "Kat isn't going anywhere

near those things. The goddamned military will take care of them."

"It's not that simple. Their skin is impenetrable. Bullets and bombs will not kill them. The only solution is to banish them. Kat has to get close enough that the dragons acknowledge her, feel her presence. Without that physical connection, the entrapment spell won't work."

"You have powers—why not just kill them yourself?" Gustavo asks.

"If we could kill them, we would have done so centuries ago when we eradicated their kindred. This is why Agatha had to imprison them."

Paula rubs her face before passing her fingers through her hair and lowering her hands to her sides. "How could Agatha do this to us? How could she just make Kat a witch without telling us? How could she let this happen?"

"I don't know!" Patricia snaps back, jolting Paula into silence. No one speaks. Everyone waits for Patricia as she inhales until her lungs are full and exhales with her eyes closed. "I don't know why Agatha chose Katarina over Jasmyn. I don't know why she didn't tell you about her decision, but it doesn't matter anymore. What matters now is controlling those dragons. Katarina, do you have the *Book of Whispers*?"

Katarina sprints upstairs and returns with it in her arms. Patricia takes the ancient book and calls Regina to give her an update while Gustavo calls his connections with local law enforcement and Fire and Rescue teams. They head out to the backyard to talk on their cell phones. Paula and Kevin hold Katarina in their arms as the reports of the dragons at the Golden Gate Bridge replay on the news channels. "She can't go near those dragons," Paula says to Kevin. "She just can't."

Filled with nervous energy, Kevin and Paula stand up and

begin cleaning up what is left of the afternoon gathering. As Paula washes casserole dishes in the sink, the refreshing sound of splashing water fills the air with a sense of normalcy, as if returning to everyday tasks was a sign of good things to come. Kevin collects small paper plates and plastic cups lying inconspicuously behind picture frames and in the dark corners of shelves. He performs the job silently as he thinks about the absurdity of his youngest daughter facing off against fire-breathing dragons. Logan folds the catering tables in the living room, slamming the legs into the inside of the table with a loud thud. Jasmyn sits at the counter and searches for online videos of the dragons on her laptop.

Katarina can't seem to will her feet into action. From their kitchen table, she stares at her mother cleaning the kitchen with the same effortlessness she sees every day and wonders how she can do anything at all. All Katarina can do is worry about how she's going to read the spell to entrap the dragons. She believes she knows how to do it; she sees Patricia's memory of how her grandmother did it, but the mere thought of intentionally casting a spell frightens her. She folds her arms tightly, hugging herself, sees that Jasmyn isn't really doing much, and walks over to her. "Jaz?" Katarina whispers, her emotions rising to the rim. "Do you…" Katarina swallows hard, "can you…"

"What is it?" Jasmyn asks monotonously without looking at her sister, staring at her laptop, still feeling the residual sting of being the scapegoat.

"Never mind," Katarina says through trembling lips. She heads toward the patio doors.

Jasmyn feels the pull dragging her toward her sister as she watches Katarina step away. *What the hell is wrong with me? I'm treating her the way Mom and Dad treat me. I'm not like them. She's my little sister, and she needs me.*

"Kat, wait."

Katarina spins around and cries out, "Why are you so mean to me? What did I ever do to make you hate me so much?"

"What are you doing to her?" Kevin shouts and runs to pick up a sobbing Katarina.

Logan is at Jasmyn's side before she knows it, pulling her back at her forearm as if she was physically attacking Katarina. "What the hell is the matter with you?"

"I didn't do anything. She started crying before I could—"

"Do you think that, for once, you could be nice to Kat? Is it really too much to ask? She has the entire world on her shoulders, and you are just bent on making it worse, aren't you?"

"I was going to—"

"I don't want to hear it." Logan pulls on her arm, dragging her further away from the kitchen and across the living room toward the front door.

Paula comes to break up the fight. "Jaz, do me a favor and just stay away from Kat. Don't talk to her, don't even look at her. You've caused enough trouble."

Jasmyn begins heaving. Sharp edges cut into her skin. She lifts her sleeves, expecting to find blood, but she sees none. *What is this pain? Am I imagining this? Am I going crazy? Do they really hate me so much that I can physically feel it?* She closes her eyes, exhales, and looks up to meet her mother's glower. The muscles in her back contract against the urge to crumple into a weakened hump. Her hand clenches her shirt at her chest as if that would keep the knives from piercing right through to her heart. She sees Logan glaring at her from behind her mother. Her father is consoling Katarina, shushing her cries, ignoring Jaz's longing gaze.

Aren't you supposed to love me unconditionally? Isn't a

mother supposed to love her children equally?

Paula exhales, shakes her head, and storms back to the counter, taking her painful vibrations with her. Jasmyn nods, accepting the unspoken answer to her questions.

"I'll be outside," she says through the sudden tightness in her throat, struggling to keep her composure, fighting off Logan's rage stabbing her body.

"Yeah, go take a long walk why don't you?" Logan says in a vicious tone. He rejoins the group in the kitchen.

In what seems like slow motion, Jasmyn takes her denim jacket off the coat rack in the foyer and puts it on. Her muscles slowly regain their strength. She steps out the front door and glances back at the rest of her family, sitting at the kitchen table, consoling Katarina, disregarding her presence. Their backs are turned toward her, shunning her from their circle, as if they have already forgotten her, as if she no longer existed.

Jasmyn walks out the front door and decides never to return.

10

DISTINCT RECOLLECTIONS

"These mortals are weak," Oxerion says with his deafening roars vibrating violently in the eardrums of any humans within earshot. His towering silhouette stands at the north entrance to the Golden Gate Bridge, emphasizing the tall stretch of his neck as it rises toward the stars. Several missiles explode against the dense skin along his back, creating clouds of gray and black smoke, yet causing no semblance of damage.

Oxerion and his minions have spent the past twelve hours traveling down the west coast, growing inch by inch, minute by minute, feeding off animals roaming the coastline forest. It was enough time for Oxerion to recall the last few days before he was sent into oblivion and the events that led him there.

He remembers how his brothers and sisters ambushed the witches during a ritual gathering at a mountain summit. It was midday in springtime. The skies were clear of winter storms, the seas glistened with sunshine, and nature lay calm and peaceful. Before the bushy hedges or the long-stemmed grass could give Agatha warning of the approaching wrath, Oxerion was already leading his army to the summit. Oxerion was the first to strike, sending a breath of fire upon the two witches nearest to him. The women burned to ashes.

Oxerion remembers watching his brothers and sisters die at the flicker of the sorceresses' hands. With a few words, the weaker, younger dragons were slain, decapitated. Counting on their love and sympathy as a weakness, Oxerion never thought the witches would lash out as quickly as they did. Though the witches were outnumbered, they were more powerful and retaliated with greater force than the dragons. The deafening roars of his siblings still echo in his head, and the debilitating look of fear in their eyes strengthens his newfound resolve.

You will pay for my brothers and sisters.

"You gave them no choice," Baronyx grumbles as he watches the one-sided visions pass through Oxerion's mind. Baronyx grimaces at his resentment toward Oxerion juxtaposed with his own guilt. He had followed his brother in his rebellion. "*We* gave them no choice."

The sickening memories of the semi-conscious state of entrapment cause Oxerion to roar. The use of black magic was rare among Finna's coven, and he'd never thought they would turn to it. He was wrong. They exercised it with all their might. He remembers Agatha standing atop a mountain, casting the dark spell, and watching Baronyx and Pterones disappear into nothingness. He remembers Agatha's face, her eyes glowing crimson as she aimed her hands at him. The vision enrages him.

He commands his mind to focus on the target. He sees the fledgling witch crying in a grown man's arms. He senses her fear and the lack of confidence she has in her magic. The image drives him forward, toward the only person who can send him back to his prison, toward the only one standing in the way of his absolute freedom. *You will pay with your kin's blood, Agatha. You will pay with her screams.*

~ ~ ~

As Baronyx crosses the rocky terrain toward the western coast, he struggles between his fond sentiments toward his mother witches and the sting of the punishment Agatha imposed upon him. He recalls Finna's wavy locks flowing down the sides of her gentle face as she encouraged him to take his first flight off a cliff. She raised him, and she and Agatha loved him. *What Oxerion did to you, Agatha, is inexcusable.*

"You did it too, Brother," Oxerion says.

With an anvil of guilt on his shoulders, Baronyx continues forward. As he and his minions cross a stretch of desert, Baronyx recalls his peaceful and painful history with the witches.

Finna brought the Gregorn Dragons into the world. The dragon eggs had been passed down for generations until they were handed to Finna by her husband's mother. They were a gift, representing hope for a long and fruitful existence. They were untouched, dormant, until Finna saw fit to give them life. She taught the dragons how to coexist with humans and other animals, how to reason and feel empathy toward other beings. Their diet consisted of plants and vegetables they harvested on the island and various fish from the shallow ocean waters. Although their appearance was menacing, the dragons never terrorized the citizens of the Isle of Enid. The human inhabitants accepted the dragons as gentle giants.

When he matured into an adult, Oxerion began to study the women of Finna's coven. He knew the dragons were immortal, he understood his siblings' strengths and weaknesses, but he needed to learn of the witches'. His grand ambitions were hidden behind the impartial countenance he maintained during his interactions with his keepers. Although he spewed his perverse utopian ideas to his brothers and sisters in private, to the witches he remained simply part of the herd. They saw nothing special in Oxerion, and Oxerion didn't want it any other way.

Unlike his older brother, Baronyx was expressive from his birth. His emotions were an open book, and as a result, the witches showed him more affection, coddling him nearly to the point of stunting his growth. He learned to fly and swim later than all the other dragons and resorted to spending more time conversing with the witches than playing with his siblings. He found the witches delightful and inspiring, and he soaked up all their lessons about respecting life, morality, and the importance of family. The witches saw a wise leader in Baronyx, even though leadership was not one of Baronyx's desires. This preference, without a doubt, vexed Oxerion.

As Finna finally grew older and weaker with mortal age, she handed over the coven's leadership to her daughter, Agatha, who continued the same practices her mother had established. When Finna was so old that she could not walk without assistance, Oxerion saw his opportunity. It was Finna's death that prompted Oxerion to gather the dragons and spark a revolution against the coven. He was so swift, so conniving that even Baronyx didn't see it coming.

The speech Oxerion gave after Finna's death sounds achingly clear in Baronyx's mind. "They control what we do, what we eat," Oxerion had said. "They believe they are stronger than us. But look at us, brothers and sisters. Look at how strong we are. We do not die. We should bow down to no one. We should hide from no one. We live on this island under the witches' control. We afford these people luxuries while we burden ourselves with their needs. We grow their food and protect their land, yet we live under their will. It is time to take our place in this world as the gods we are!" Oxerion stirred passion in his sibling dragons, a sense of purpose and destiny. They rose up and attacked the coven.

"And for what, Oxerion?" Baronyx now grumbles into the night air. "Because the witches controlled where we went, dictated what we ate, and required us to work the land alongside them? I would not call it weakness. Finna loved us. The witches loved us. They cared for us as if we were their children."

Instead of acknowledging Baronyx's memories, Oxerion decides to produce his own images of the past, his version of the histories that pain him so that Baronyx can see his reasoning. Oxerion recalls when Agatha crushed a younger dragon under the weight of thousand-ton boulders. "She could have spared Mardyn!" Oxerion shouts. "He was not strong enough to cause any real damage, yet she destroyed him."

Baronyx remembers the gray dragon. Though Mardyn was older than Baronyx, he was only half his size and possessed a childlike innocence. "He tried to slice Agatha's head off with his razor-edged tail. She had to kill him." He shakes his head until the memory fades. "He would never have attacked her if you hadn't—"

"Inspired him, encouraged him to stand up for himself and to fight for something all his own?" Oxerion huffs, and clouds of smoke rise from his nostrils.

"He was fighting for you and no one else!" Baronyx shakes his enormous head and trudges onward, trying to erase the putrid visions from his mind.

Oxerion recalls another memory, when Inga froze his weaker brethren in midair and slammed them against the mountainside, shattering them into a million pieces. Baronyx remembers that attack well. A burst of fire from his snout killed Inga faster than he'd expected.

"They didn't deserve to die," Baronyx wails at Oxerion. "Mardyn, Inga…none of them deserved their end."

"The witches killed our family. You were defending your own!"

"They didn't deserve our betrayal." Baronyx spits to the side before spraying fire from his snout toward, but not directly at, the men and machines that attempt to interrupt his march. Humans, as Baronyx has recently learned, are not easily driven away by blazing fire. In fact, it antagonizes them. This weighs heavy on Baronyx's heart. He isn't trying to provoke such a reaction. "They are acting in self-defense. They think we are a menace. Your actions, Oxerion, are going to be the end of us. We should be trying to make amends, not chaos."

"You sentimental fool!" Oxerion growls. "They want to kill you!"

Baronyx sighs. "They can't kill us, Brother. They can't even scratch the weak points around our ankles and throats. They are no threat to us."

"They want to destroy us!" Oxerion catches a few seagulls in his snout as he crosses the San Francisco Bay.

"They are scared out of their wits."

After a low chuckle, Pterones says. "Yes, but their bones are just as succulent as I remember. I feasted on a cabin full of them. I am about to roast those in the flying machines." Pterones opens his mouth wide and clamps down on the helicopter cabin, crushing two military men in the gruesome process. Missiles explode outside his mouth as he sucks the carcasses through the bent metal.

The vision causes a sinking sensation inside Baronyx's stomach. "They are thinking, reasoning creatures, Pterones! You cannot eat them!"

His brother spits out the metal remains of the chopper, like a baby back rib devoid of meat. "I beg to differ."

Oxerion bites into the first few belts holding up the Golden Gate Bridge and rips them up from the base. Multiple rope lines snap, causing the bridge to dance across the bay. The eerie sound of bending metal echoes across several miles until the bridge breaks in half. Cars slide into the bay. Oxerion spits flame onto the waves, and people are thrown to their deaths in the fiery waters.

Baronyx releases an agonized growl, unable to do anything to control his brothers' actions. "The coven acted in self-defense, Oxerion. They knew you would lead the pack to other parts of the world and kill every living thing in your path. You tore off the wings of the kragars and murdered them; you convinced our brothers and sisters to pull the chocrins out of the sea and tear them to pieces. You were killing and eating the humans on the island. What were the witches supposed to do? You may still have Pterones convinced, but I stopped believing in your goals the instant you attacked them. The witches never did anything to us."

When he reaches the beach, Oxerion turns his mighty head back to gaze at the glory of his destruction. Flames reflect in his pensive eyes. "They created us, Brother, with unparalleled strength and power."

And compassion. Baronyx chest fills with sorrow as he sees what Oxerion sees - the mangled bridge, the explosions, the devastation.

"Compassion!" Oxerion huffs. "Your principles don't matter do they, dear Brother? Agatha trapped you in oblivion with us. She ignored your pleas to give us another chance."

"They had every right to entrap us. I don't blame them. I blame you. You sacrificed us all for your selfish goals."

"Selfish goals indeed! I wanted our freedom."

"At what cost? Death is not freedom!" Baronyx blows flames into the air, away from the helicopters, and stomps down on the mountainside, causing a tremor across a handful of cities. He marches on, each step heavy with frustration. "We three survived because Finna had given us a magical shield. Otherwise we would have died along with everyone else you sacrificed for your cause. I want this to end. I want us to live peacefully like we did before your revolution. That is worth sacrificing for."

Uncertain if he had understood Baronyx's words

correctly, Pterones stops chewing on his meal. His minions halt by his side, awaiting orders.

Oxerion snarls. "And when the moment comes…will you sacrifice me for your cause, Brother?"

The rumbles cease when Baronyx stops short. Would he hand over his life? Would he sacrifice his life or his brother's life to save mankind? Would he sacrifice Katarina so that he and his brothers could live? What is life now, with only his two brothers, when no one else on the planet cares about them? He once felt love and understanding from the coven; now he only feels contempt toward Oxerion.

Oxerion huffs when he realizes where Baronyx's thoughts are headed.

"We have to find Katarina and reason with her. She can send us somewhere safe, where no one will attack us, where everyone will leave us alone to live until the end of the earth. We can earn her trust."

"Indeed," Oxerion says as another missile explodes against his chest. He breathes fire at the offending helicopter, sending it to its demise. "Let us reason with those that want us dead."

Reasoning is not Pterones' strong suit, and any attempt would detract from whatever he is eating, which, at the moment, is an elk he picked up at a local zoo. But he can sense pain in Baronyx's voice. He decides to consider Baronyx's argument silently.

Baronyx raises his tired shoulders, stretches out his weary wings, and flaps once before feeling the strain along his jagged spine. His wing muscles aren't strong enough to lift his body into the air just yet; he takes comfort in knowing his brothers have the same problem. "You will not destroy our only chance at a peaceful coexistence," he says, picking up the pace.

"So you will go against me in battle then, will you?"

Baronyx does not respond.

Food lodges itself in Pterones's esophagus when he tries to swallow.

"So be it," Oxerion says. He turns back to blow a long stream of fire at what's left of the Golden Gate Bridge until it is covered in flames and smoke.

11

POWERLESS

Elemental Spells ~ *Elemental spells manipulate natural elements as desired. This spell requires the usage of the caster's physical energy. The amount of energy consumed may render the caster weak and vulnerable to the influences of darkness. The conjurer must be aware of the potential consequences to herself if using such magic.*

Below is a list of elemental spells:

...

Controlling Spells ~ *Controlling spells control the physical awareness, the consciousness, of a living thing. This spell manipulates the mind and requires the usage of the caster's physical energy. The amount of energy consumed may render the caster weak and vulnerable to the influences of darkness. The conjurer must be aware of the potential consequences to herself if using such magic.*

Below is a list of controlling spells and their counterspells:

...

Entrapment Spells ~ *Entrapment spells send living things into a supernatural prison located within the intersecting dimensions of time and space. The target will no longer be in the physical world. Only a sorceress of a particular bloodline is capable of conducting entrapment spells. The sorceress must make the victim aware of her presence and intention. This awareness allows the caster to acknowledge the severity of what she is about to do to her victim, the cruelty of the magic and its consequences. An entrapment case is required for entrapment spells. This spell requires manipulation of the mind and spirit against the victim's will and is, therefore, purely dark in nature. The conjurer must be aware of the consequences to herself if using such magic.*

Below is a list of entrapment spells and their counterspells:

...

Entrapment Cases *~ Entrapment cases are physical representations of the prison holding the target of an executed entrapment spell. Since the prison chamber lies in another realm, the token is used to remind the caster of its existence. The material, the size, and the shape of the container do not matter. The only physical requirement is that it can be opened and closed. Only the sorceress who casts the spell, or a sorceress of her bloodline, can relinquish the enchantment and release its prisoners. Once a sorceress consecrates an entrapment case, it is indestructible through natural forces. Only magic can destroy it.*

~ ~ ~

With the *Book of Whispers* open and resting on her thighs, Patricia re-reads the ancient rules and wonders again how Jasmyn destroyed the enchanted relic. *The gift can only be passed to one female. So, Katarina must have read another spell to weaken the box's enchantment.* Patricia sanctifies the box Katarina fetched for her, a wooden ivory case with metal latches and red and pink roses painted on its flat sides—a stark contrast to the box she remembers.

Gustavo finishes a call on his cell phone and approaches Patricia. "Walter, a friend of mine who works with my First Response Unit, has his helicopter at the airport. His chopper has loud speakers we can use to get the dragons' attention. He's a veteran helicopter pilot, and he's won a ton of awards for his flight skills, so he will be able to keep us a safe distance from the dragons."

"He agreed to fly for us, to get us close to the dragons?" Patricia asks.

"Well, not exactly. I asked him to meet me at the airport and to get his chopper fired up. But…I know him. I've known him forever. Once we explain the situation and tell him we need his help, he'll help us."

Patricia nods. She hopes he's judged his friend correctly. Noble auras do tend to attract other noble auras, after all.

"The chopper has enough room for five. The pilot, co-pilot (that's me), Katarina, and two more adults."

"I still don't understand why Katarina has to go up there." Kevin rubs his forehead.

"These kinds of dark spells require a physical connection between the sorceress and the target," Patricia says as Katarina leans on her arm on the kitchen counter and stares off into the distance. "Being in each other's presence creates a bond, a connection, even though they are not touching. Think about how different it is when you talk to someone over video chat and when you talk to someone in the same room. You can feel their presence. You sense their energy, their life force."

Kevin's eyes widen. "The dragons will feel her presence? They'll know she's in the helicopter?"

Patricia nods.

"Then I'm going with her."

"Me too." Paula puts on her blue sweatshirt.

"There isn't enough room. I need to be with Katarina, in case…"

Paula freezes. "In case what?"

"In case it doesn't work, and we have to think of something else."

"Why wouldn't it work?" Paula's hands ball into fists at her side. "You have the box. You have the spell. You have Agatha's granddaughter, the next witch in your goddamned coven. Why wouldn't it work?"

"Katarina is the youngest witch I've ever known to exist. There are physical and emotional requirements to practicing sorcery that adults naturally possess and children don't. This is why the gift is passed on only when the successor is of a mature age." Patricia watches Paula shake her head and look away in disbelief. She feels equally frustrated. "I'm not one hundred percent certain this will work. And if it doesn't, I might have to buy us more time to figure out what to do next."

Paula shakes her head. "This is unbelievable. You want to risk my daughter's life!"

"I don't have time to explain everything right now. We have to get to the dragons while they can't fly. They are still relatively weak from centuries of entrapment, but once they grow stronger and their wings become fully functional, everything gets harder."

Visions of flying beasts invade Paula's thoughts. With tears welling up in her eyes, she nods, swallowing through the rock in her throat, and walks over to Kevin for a comforting embrace.

He kisses his wife on the head. "I'll go with them. I'll keep Katarina safe."

"I know you will," Paula whispers before sitting with Katarina at the counter, wrapping her arms around her shoulders, kissing her cheeks, and telling her what a brave little girl she is.

But brave is the last thing Katarina feels; she feels guilt. She doesn't know why she screamed out the way she did earlier and got Jasmyn in so much trouble that even Logan reproached her. Logan never scolded Jasmyn so severely, at least not that Katarina had ever seen. She scans the room for her older sister and feels a sense of emptiness. The physical sensation of her absence perplexes Katarina, and she wonders if that's also part of being a witch. Mostly, though, she just wants her sister, even if her sister doesn't want her.

"Mom," Katarina whispers. "Where's Jaz?"

"I don't know, sweetheart." Paula wipes tears from her cheek with her sweatshirt sleeve.

Logan joins their huddle.

"Do you think she'll be proud of me?"

"Of course she will," Logan says. "She's already proud of you. She just has a hard time showing it."

"Deep down in China, huh?"

Logan smiles sadly. "Way deep down in China." He winks at his mother who stares at them with a perplexed look on her face. "Private joke, Mom."

"Yeah Mom. Private joke."

~ ~ ~

As everyone climbs into Gustavo's pickup truck, Gustavo sees the family across the street loading a blue sedan with luggage, bags of food, and boxes of other belongings. A woman secures a baby into a booster chair in the backseat while her husband loads diapers and formula into the trunk. Gustavo turns on the engine and looks over at Patricia. "What are we going to do if the spell doesn't work?"

After the driver's door is slammed shut, the blue sedan pulls backwards out of the driveway, and upon turning onto the road, it backs into a rose bush and knocks over a stretch of white picket fence lining the neighbor's front yard. The tires squeal as the car pulls forward and drives away.

A patch of dryness in Patricia's throat makes her swallow as she watches the car turn the corner. "I'm working on it."

Once on the highway, Gustavo drives his truck off onto the right shoulder to avoid rows of cars stuck in slow-moving traffic. Several drivers follow his lead, and soon the makeshift lane gets too congested, and Gustavo is barely moving. He mounts a Bull Blaster on top of his truck and activates its spinning red and blue lights and emergency siren. He picks up a small device and speaks into it. "Please keep this lane open for emergency vehicles. I repeat, this lane is for emergency vehicles only. Please move to your left."

Slowly, with honks reverberating from all lanes, the cars in front of him make room. As he passes and people scan the Fire & Rescue decals on the side of his red truck, the honks diminish. Gustavo shakes his head as he wonders what he would have done if he didn't have a Fire & Rescue truck today. He wonders if Walter will be able to get to the airport in the chaotic traffic, but then he remembers Walter also drives a Fire & Rescue truck during the week. *Good thing none of this happened on the weekend.*

Gustavo puts on the local radio station and whispers "holy shit" when a reporter says that close to a hundred thousand people are estimated to have perished in the wake of the black dragon's destruction of the Golden Gate Bridge and its passage through Marin County and San Francisco.

"A hundred thousand people..." Kevin whispers incredulously from the back seat. He holds onto Katarina more tightly.

When the reporter announces the neighborhoods that have been burned and crushed by the black dragon and his minions,

Kevin recognizes them as neighborhoods that cut through the middle of the peninsula. If it stays on track, the dragon may come close to his home. He calls Paula and tells her to prepare to leave with Jasmyn and Logan, to head to the coastline where many survivors have been fleeing out of the black dragon's path of destruction. While on the phone, Kevin glances behind and sees a fiery orange cloud of smoke rising into the night sky, just as the reporter describes.

When the reporter continues about the other two dragons heading toward the bay area, Gustavo lowers the volume and asks, "What's the story with the other dragons? Why are they heading for San Francisco?"

Rubbing her eyelids, Patricia takes a moment to formulate her thoughts. "The black dragon is Oxerion, the leader. Pterones is green, and the red one is called Baronyx. Finna, Agatha's mother, created the dragons with her blood. The dragons are drawn to their own blood, and that includes Katarina. They also know only Finna's bloodline has the power to entrap them. They probably want her dead."

Kevin barely reacts to this latest development. There is only so much shock a single person can feel before he becomes numb to all bad news. He strokes his fingers through Katarina's hair as she rests her head on his lap.

Patricia turns around in her seat to face Kevin. "We'll fix this. We've done it before."

Air stings his lungs as Kevin takes the deepest breath of his life. He grimaces at the horrific image in his mind—a bloody, lifeless Katarina lying in his arms. To fight off the horrendous vision, he shuts his eyes and concentrates on happier memories, of when five-year-old Katarina learned to ride her rainbow bicycle, yellow streamers hanging from the handlebars. Even after falling and scraping her right knee, elbow, and shoulder, Katarina never gave up. It took almost two months before she finally got the hang of it. A minute later he recalls the time Katarina convinced him that she was strong enough to swim in the deep end of the town pool. Anxious, he watched Katarina as she struggled to swim toward the edge, splashing and dipping. He was ready to jump in if she needed help, but she never did. She never gave up. The weakness he feared Katarina would develop because of the heart condition she was born with never manifested, at least not in her spirit.

He searches for more heroic moments in the hopes that they are predictors of today's outcome. They are evidence of Katarina's inner strength; she can cross any obstacle, overcome any adversity, and even defeat giant dragons.

After twenty more minutes of calamitous traffic, Gustavo finally drives into San Carlos Airport. Walter, Gustavo's lifelong best friend, had them cleared to enter the airport. He meets them at the gate to escort them inside.

"Why are you wearing a monkey suit?" Walter asks as he shakes Gustavo's hand.

"Paula's mother-in-law died. Today was the funeral."

"Oh. Sorry man." He leans in to give Kevin a tight hug, pounding his back. "My condolences." He turns back to Gustavo. "Gus, everyone has been grounded because of those dragons. Airspace is open to military only."

Gustavo steps closer to Walter. "Those dragons are after my niece. They're killing thousands of people and setting everything on fire just to get to her."

Jerking his head back in surprise, Walter glances at Katarina and then back at Gustavo. "I'm sorry, Gus. There's nothing I can do. I tried to get clearance, but I can't get high enough up the chain of command. The military has taken over everything, and I don't have the authority to—"

Patricia gently tugs on Gustavo's arm, pulling him a step behind her. She stares straight into Walter's eyes and curves the right side of her lips upwards. "Walter, please be a gentleman and take us to your helicopter."

Without further argument, Walter turns on his toes and starts walking. Patricia winks at Gustavo as they follow.

"That's a useful trick," Gustavo whispers.

"It comes in handy."

"Promise you won't use that on me."

"I promise." She keeps her eyes on Walter's back and suppresses a smile.

Walter heads to his helicopter stationed at a hangar close to the riverbed at the end of the airport. The helicopter blades start spinning as soon as Kevin, Katarina, and Patricia climb into the back seat.

A shrieking Katarina points out the left side of the chopper. "It's the red dragon!"

"Go!" Gustavo yells the instant he slides the door shut.

The helicopter blades are at full speed, and Walter lifts the helicopter into the air without warning. Katarina nearly jerks out of her loose-fitting seat belt, but Kevin grabs hold of her arms.

As Gustavo instructs Walter to hover high above the dragon, he notices the dragon is not approaching them. The smaller, humanoid monsters at his feet are walking along the airport lanes, clearing a path. To Gustavo, it seems the dragon is trying to walk around the planes and vehicles.

"What is it doing?" Walter asks into the headset.

"I don't know," Gustavo replies, gulping hard. They watch in awe as the red dragon turns its mighty head upwards toward the chopper. It keeps its snout shut and releases a puff of smoke through its cavernous nostrils.

After a moment, Katarina speaks into her headset.

"Baronyx says he's not going to harm us. He doesn't want to hurt us."

Gustavo, Patricia, and Kevin all look at Katarina with their eyes wide open.

"You can communicate with him?" Patricia asks.

"Yes. He says he tried to walk around the humans and not crush anything. He told his minions to eat only small animals, and to leave the humans alone. He doesn't want any trouble. He wants to make amends. He says he's sorry."

"Don't listen to him, Katarina. He is a creature of magic, with his own powers of manipulation." Patricia points to a page in the *Book of Whispers*. "You have to read this spell."

"But he says he—"

"I don't care what he says. He is trying to persuade you to *not* put him back into captivity. He will say anything."

Kevin grabs Katarina's hand. "Kat, these dragons have killed thousands of innocent people. You have to stop them."

"But he's not the one killing," Katarina says. "The other one is."

Patricia leans closer to Katarina. "It doesn't matter. They are brothers. They will destroy this earth and everyone on it. Try to recall our memories. They killed our sisters. They attacked us without provocation. They betrayed all of us centuries ago, and they will betray you now."

"Gus, we have to decide on a plan of action," Walter says into the headset. "If this thing blows fire at us, we're toast."

Patricia takes a deep breath and places the *Book of Whispers* in Katarina's lap. "Walter, turn on the speakers. She's about to read the spell."

Katarina looks to her father for guidance. She senses his strength and determination as his arms hug her shoulders. "I am the only one who can stop them," she says weakly, gazing up at him with sorrowful eyes.

Kevin nods and squeezes her tighter.

With conflicting emotions, and with reluctance weighing heavy on her heart, she accepts her task. Katarina slowly reads the words from the *Book of Whispers*:

> Encased in fire and ice
> To sleep you will be
> Between yesterday and tomorrow,
> Within here and there,
> Everywhere will be nowhere.
> Trapped for eternity.

The world around Katarina seems to have gone silent as she opens the newly enchanted wooden case, Baronyx's new prison, and closes it just as Patricia had instructed. Baronyx bows his head and slumps his shoulders as he waits for the spell to execute.

But, to his surprise, nothing happens.

12

NARROW ESCAPES

Tears spill down Katarina's cheeks as she repeats the spell twice more at Patricia's request, each instance throwing a spear at Baronyx's heart. Her soft voice soon fades into weak whimpers so that when Katarina recites the spell once more, heaving sobs between each verse, her voice becomes almost unrecognizable.

"She would banish you ten times over if she could," Oxerion says, growling up at the sky.

"The spell has no effect on me."

"And you wish it did? Do you want to go back to that hell?"

Baronyx releases a loud roar, temporarily knocking a helicopter off balance with the wind from his powerful breath. "I want all of this killing to end!"

"And you tried, Brother. You tried. But they will not listen to any reasoning."

"She is just a little girl, Oxerion. She may not understand my meaning."

On a rolling San Francisco hill, not too far in the distance, Oxerion stands tall and stretches his back muscles. He is finally able to flap his wings and lift his body off the ground. "They will never give up on destroying us."

Feeling helpless, Baronyx looks down upon his minions and sits in a slump in the middle of the airport runway. The minions slouch down next to Baronyx, reflecting their leader's disposition. From the viewpoint of the dozens of soldiers at the airport and news helicopters in the sky, it seems Katarina's voice forced the giant beast and his army into submission.

"I'm sorry, Baronyx," Katarina whimpers to herself.

As Patricia speaks to Regina on the phone and decides on their next course of action, Katarina whispers, "Trapped for eternity," understanding its full meaning. *Can you hear me, Baronyx?*

Baronyx lifts his head up to look at her. *I am listening, Katarina.*

She gasps and continues her conversation with Baronyx in secret, fearing Patricia will try to force her to do or say something she doesn't want to. *I don't want to put you away, Baronyx, but the other dragons are killing a lot of people.*

I understand. It's our own fault. We brought this upon ourselves.

Can you stop them from killing people?

Baronyx lowers his head once more. *I cannot.*

Then what can we do, Baronyx? Tell me what I can do to stop them.

Katarina's innocent voice is so full of trust, so full of courage that Baronyx's eyes widen with optimism. *You can trust me.*

Katarina wipes her face and nods. *I do trust you.*

In feeling Agatha's love near him as he hasn't felt in so long, and in hearing the trust and bravery emanating from the little girl's inner voice, a refreshing sense of determination urges Baronyx to his feet. He looks squarely at the helicopter. *I will not let them hurt you, sweet Katarina. I swear it. Out of respect for Finna and Agatha, your kin, my sweet mothers, I will not let my brothers hurt you.*

~ ~ ~

"Gus," Walter says into the headset while gesturing toward the north at a black figure moving across the evening sky, "is that what I think it is?"

Oxerion appears over the terminal in wobbled flight, heading for the helicopter. He glides in an uncoordinated pattern on stiff, rickety wings, but he is still able to blow flames at Walter's helicopter. With Walter's expert handle of the controls, the fire misses them by a few feet.

The concrete floor of the runway crackles the instant Oxerion crashes into the ground. He roars in anger, breathes fire on everything around him, and orders his minions to trample and kill everything in their path. Baronyx launches his red titanic body at the black beast, resolute to keep his promise.

The two dragons gnarl and claw at each other, baring their sharp teeth. Their long, charcoal nails scratch the leather surface of their skins, slicing the thick scales. Fire roars across the sky and on the ground below, creating plumes of thick gray smoke rising into the night. Oxerion flaps his weak wings clumsily, and they betray him often enough that Baronyx uses them to his advantage. With all his weight, Baronyx clasps his claws onto his older brother's limbs and pulls him down to the earth, disrupting his momentum.

"He's fighting him off!" Katarina shouts. "Baronyx is fighting Oxerion!"

Everyone watches the colossal battle as Walter rises to a safe distance.

"I don't understand." Patricia says into the headset.

Another blaze of fire spews dangerously close to the helicopter blades, and Walter jerks the handles backwards. "The spell didn't work. We can't just stay in the air. I know a port down south we can make in ten minutes."

"We can't land around here. How far inland can you fly?" Patricia shouts.

"On this bird? It's got a full tank. I can make it to Nevada. Anything further, and I need to stop and refuel."

"I'll buy us some time."

A red glimmer shines from Patricia's eyes as she mutters foreign words under her breath. She extends her fingers out in a circular fashion, as if wrapping them around an invisible ball on her lap. Gustavo, Katarina, and Kevin watch as a silver glow surrounds Patricia, illuminating her frame in the back of the helicopter. She repeats the controlling spell three times, with each instance her tone growing angrier as if her stern voice will force the spell to execute. While her muscles weaken and her hands struggle to keep their fingers stretched out over the imaginary orb, Patricia reads the spell one more time, almost shouting, and the two dragons finally fall asleep.

After she finishes speaking and the radiance around her diminishes, she drops her arms and leans back in her seat. She breathes erratically as sweat drips down her forehead. "We need to get out into the desert," she says in a strained voice, her face wincing at the onslaught of nausea. "Go somewhere where the dragons won't cause any more deaths, and where Regina and I can fight them without worrying about killing people, until we figure out what to do." Bile creeps up her throat. Patricia bends forward and swallows hard. Though Kevin places his hand on her back, trying to calm her heaving, she waves him off. "Regina is stuck in Mississippi somewhere. I need her here with me. The dragons will be sleeping for only a few hours."

Walter turns eastward and picks up speed. He glances at Gustavo. "I'll call my father when we get to the base."

~ ~ ~

Major Brigante and his wife had gone to sleep just after dinner, around seven in the evening, as had been the custom in his home for several years now. He wasn't aware of the catastrophe on the other side of the country. No one from his command post in Camp LeJeune in Jacksonville, North Carolina has contacted him yet. When the phone stirred him awake, Major Brigante was in his third dream.

"A magic spell?" Major Ernesto Brigante shouts into his phone as he walks to the bathroom to wash his face. "Walter, please, it's five in the morning. You're waking me up for fairy tales?"

But Walter sounds edgy, and Ernesto decides not to hang up on his son until after he explains himself. He listens to Walter's fantastic story of dragons and witches, and the hairs on Ernesto's arms and back stiffen.

"Walter, do you hear yourself? You sound like you've lost your mind. You sound like you did when you got back from Afghanistan." Ernesto takes a deep breath and rubs his forehead as he quickly recalls all the funerals, memorials, and cemetery visits he and Walter attended. On every car ride to one of the sorrowful events, Walter would curse under his breath about losing his entire platoon, about being the sole survivor, and bang his fist on the passenger side dashboard. His voice now sounds like his voice then, full of desperation. Ernesto swallows hard, fearing his son is experiencing some sort of delayed post-traumatic stress disorder.

"Dad, I'm not going crazy. This is real."

Rushing to the other room so his wife doesn't hear, Earnesto whispers, "Son, I haven't received any calls about," Earnesto rolls his eyes, "witches or dragons. Please, stop this nonsense."

"You don't have to believe me. Turn on the TV. It's all over the news."

After Ernesto watches just five minutes of the incredible news on television, the reporter presents a video of a helicopter flying close to the dragons at San Carlos Airport. "Is that you in the helicopter?" Ernesto asks with a knot in his throat.

"Yes, sir," Walter says calmly, no longer shouting.

A blend of fear and pride overcomes Ernesto as the footage replays on the news channel, the reporter remarking on the pilot's exceptional skill at avoiding the flames and keeping the chopper's flight steady amidst the pandemonium. A man in a decorated uniform sitting next to a news reporter states, "The reason those civilians are flying so close to the dragons is unknown."

"Wow," the reporter says, gasping as the footage shows the helicopter narrowly avoiding flames from the dragon's mouth. "That's some pilot."'

A few more minutes pass before Walter continues in the most serious tone Ernesto has ever heard from his son. "I really need your help."

Major Ernesto Brigante clears his throat. "Son, I'll do what I can. Tell me what you need."

~ ~ ~

"My father's team picked Regina up in Mississippi. She'll be here in less than three hours," Walter says after speaking to an officer at Fallon Naval Air Station in Nevada. He walks into a conference room assigned to him and his guests and stands next to Patricia and Gustavo as they stare at a flat screen television mounted on the wall. Crashes, roars, and explosions blast from the

TV as the news replays the scene that ends with the giant beasts falling on top of one another in a comatose state.

"Good. The sleep spell will only last a few more hours." Patricia rubs her arms and shoulders.

"Are you sore from casting that spell?" Gustavo asks.

"They're enormous beasts. It takes more strength than I'm used to. It's been a long while since I've used controlling spells."

Walter exhales as he watches the screen. "Even in their sleep, our weapons are useless. Look at them."

Gustavo, Patricia, and Walter all shake their heads as the live footage at San Carlos Airport unravels like a scene from *Gulliver's Travels*. The military attempts to restrain the dragons using copious numbers of cargo nets and tranquilizing gases.

"We should all get some rest," Gustavo says, his tired voice matching the look on his face.

Walter takes refuge in a corner of the conference room with his worn, coffee-stained sweater bundled into a pillow. Atop a pile of thick, wiry blankets stacked up to three feet high, Katarina lies asleep with her head on Kevin's suit jacket. In a seated position next to Katarina's bed, leaning his back against the wall with his right arm resting on his right knee, Kevin drifts between consciousness and slumber. Gustavo sits back in one of the chairs around a small round table and watches Patricia pace back and forth.

Without warning, Patricia rushes out of the conference room before anyone notices frustration taking hold of her. She paces back and forth in a zigzag pattern while muttering incoherent ideas and thoughts that intersect in her mind. She rubs her eyelids and forehead as she tries to figure out what to do next. When Gustavo appears before her in the hallway, she shakes her head. "I don't understand," she says to Gustavo while rubbing her knuckles. "The spell should have worked. We did everything

Agatha did three centuries ago. I remember it distinctly. She opened the box, said the words, closed it."

"What do you mean 'you remember it'?"

Patricia stops pacing as the cyclone of her thoughts suddenly pauses. She glances at Gustavo as he shuts his eyes, the epiphany finally dawning on him.

"You're three hundred years old too, aren't you?"

"Three hundred ninety-nine, actually."

He smirks. "Why haven't you aged? Agatha was an old woman."

Patricia spots a vending machine down the hallway and walks toward it. While gazing at the potato chips and chocolate bars, she explains that immortality is broken when a witch gives birth to a child. She keeps her eyes on the machine until she finishes. "It's nature's way of keeping balance."

"So…you have children and now you have to die? How is that balance?"

"Imagine if all witches with this kind of power had lots of children, all of them inheriting her magic, and then imagine they are immortal."

Gustavo lifts his chin. "The world would be a different place."

"Right. So, it seems Mother Nature decided to place limitations on both our immortality and on who can inherit our gift; which, in my opinion, was a pretty smart move. There is a lot of evil in the world."

"So, only one woman down your family tree can inherit the gift, and your mortality starts the moment you have children— all in an effort to control the amount of supernatural magic in the world."

"That's the theory."

Gustavo leans against the edge of the vending machine.

"Are only women capable of having this power?"

The dollar bill in Patricia's hand feels crisp as she unfolds it. "There are male sorcerers too, from other clans, with similar limitations. Men can only pass on their gifts to male family members. Women can only pass their gift to women."

He tries to filter the dozens of questions floating in his mind, the list growing with each answer. "So, what kinds of powers do you have? You made Walter shut up and take us to his chopper without question, so I know you can manipulate people." Gustavo narrows his eyes. "Which makes me wonder why you didn't just manipulate Paula into believing you."

"Just because you have the ability doesn't mean you should use it. I use it only when it's necessary and it does little harm, like," Patricia takes a deep breath, "when I made you believe Katarina had a fainting spell."

Gustavo creases his eyebrows.

"I needed you to calm everyone else down, so I made you believe it was a simple fainting spell and nothing more. I needed time to figure out what to do."

With his lips pressed tightly, Gustavo lowers his gaze.

"As for Paula, I needed her to trust me, to really trust me, and you can't get that with mental manipulation." She shakes her head. "Nothing good comes from lies. Look at all that's happened because of Agatha's secret. If she had been completely honest with her family, none of this would have ever happened."

He nods. "So you haven't manipulated anyone since?"

"No." Patricia gives a mischievous smile. Gustavo matches it. "You're just going to have to trust me."

"Or you'll turn me to ice?"

"Exactly."

Gustavo chuckles at the ludicrous reality of the conversation and at Patricia's lighthearted tone. His perception of witches stems from childhood stories, movies, and Halloween costumes; the image is nothing like the woman standing in front of him. He senses her frankness, and he can't help but take advantage of Patricia's momentary offering and ask for more. "Tell me about you and Agatha. Why didn't you stay together?"

Though Patricia stayed away at Agatha's request, she feels that answer is inadequate. They were both at fault, at the very least, with her sharing more of the blame than Agatha. "She had children. She was mortal. She wanted to keep her magic a secret. I couldn't stay." Her voice betrays her, cracking at the last word, and she lowers her stare in hopes that Gustavo will take the hint.

He does.

After few silent moments, he asks about the details of the battle with the dragons centuries ago, about the other witches, and Patricia answers his questions as best she can with the patience of a professor lecturing a willing student. Their eyes are in a comfortable lock on each other as Gustavo slowly breaks down Patricia's guard. He's not frightened, as almost every man who ever had a clue about Patricia was; he wants to know more, not less.

"What about your family? Do you stay in touch with them?"

Patricia lowers her gaze once more. "I haven't kept tabs on my family in centuries." She recalls the sight of her grandnephews dying. "It's too painful."

"You've been alone all this time?"

Patricia nods, glancing at the vending machine buttons, feeling unaccustomed to this openness about her past. She suddenly feels like a specimen being probed, like a newly discovered species of insect studied by an entomologist. She can feel Gustavo's stare burning her, but she can't decipher if he is interested in her as a witch or interested in her.

"And you've never wanted children?"

The glare coming from Patricia makes Gustavo aware that he crossed a personal boundary.

"I'm sorry," Gustavo says after a few awkward seconds. "You don't have to answer that. That was intrusive of me."

"No, that's alright. It's an understandable question coming from a mortal who has probably lived a privileged life." She faces the machine casually, puts in the dollar bill, and selects her Peanut M&M's. She recalls Agatha asking her a similar question. She had felt just as offended.

"Forget I asked."

"No. Let's entertain the question. You're asking me why I would choose not to have a family and do the normal female thing and procreate. This is, after all, what women were made for, right? We are meant to be gentle, kind, motherly, have tons of babies, and—"

"I was just wondering…" Gustavo says, raising his voice.

"Wondering what?"

A deep crease appears on Gustavo's forehead. "If you were the kind of woman who would give up family for power. Now I know."

She presses her lips together and narrows her eyes at him. "You have no idea the kind of woman I am, or what I am capable of. When you have lived hundreds of years and seen everyone you love die before your eyes, and when you have witnessed worse atrocities than what you may have seen in hundreds of movies, with the screams of the dead echoing in your head for decades…" Patricia stops her tirade, takes a deep breath, and steps away from Gustavo.

Regretting his intrusion, Gustavo stuffs his hands into his pockets and clears his throat. "I'm sorry," he says, his voice unusually hoarse. "That was an asshole thing for me to say. You are here, with my family, trying to fix what Agatha broke, and here I am passing judgment on you." Without looking up at Patricia, Gustavo turns and heads back to the conference room.

As he walks away, Patricia closes her eyes and takes a deep, shuddering breath.

13

LOST & FOUND

When Jasmyn took her mother's car, she didn't have a destination in mind. Through tears of resentment, she drove onto I-280 and into the night. When she saw the sign that led to her childhood home, she was reminded of a special moment with her grandmother, of the day Jasmyn started kindergarten. A rainy day and thick mud secured a fall in the schoolyard, in front of her new classmates, and teasing throughout her first day of school. When her grandmother picked her up at the end of the day, Jasmyn was still crying.

"These kids don't know what you are truly made of. All they see is messy hair, dirty clothes, and a careless trip in the mud, and they miss out on everything else," her grandmother had said as she wiped her eyes. "They have no idea how special you are." Reassurance from her grandmother that she wasn't a freak as everyone claimed was all she needed to stop crying. She hasn't experienced that kind of tenderness from anyone in her family in years.

After taking the exit, she felt an overwhelming sense of exhaustion. She was tired—from driving, from being angry, from her family's dismissal, from everything. Sleep was in desperate order, so she pulled into a lit parking lot and turned off the car. As every mechanical sound stopped, her mind replayed the memory again. Her grandmother's voice was as clear as if she was speaking to her from the passenger seat. Jasmyn tried shaking it away, tried thinking about something else, but the memory kept repeating itself, each instance growing richer with detail, down to her grandmother's caramel moccasins and the graying bun held in place with a dozen hair pins.

I don't want to cry anymore, Nana. Please get out of my head. Jasmyn leaned back in the driver's seat, pressed her eyes shut, and her bitterness floated away in the embers of the moment, and all she was left with was a sweet memory to dream about.

~ ~ ~

"What do you mean she didn't come home last night? It's seven in the morning," Kevin whispers into his cell phone, out in the hallway. "Where the hell is she?"

Paula walks back and forth in her kitchen, her hand rubbing her eyebrows. "I don't know. Logan just went out to look for her. She's not answering her cell phone. Even Logan is surprised she didn't come home. And there are these giant monsters all over the place that have been..." Her voice catches, and she winces at the possibilities. The news has been replaying not only the dragon battle but also the gory scenes on the ground as Oxerion's minions pass through unsuspecting neighborhoods feeding on anything in sight. As they overeat and outgrow the limits of their form, they split into two creatures straight down the middle of their spine and restart their growth pattern. The obedient beings are multiplying, just as Oxerion wishes.

"Don't think like that, Paula," Kevin says in a shaky voice. "She's fine. She has to be."

"It's all my fault. She ran off because I yelled at her."

"We all yelled at her," Kevin says.

She stops in front of her refrigerator and gazes at a family photo from when Katarina was born, its edges worn from years of up-close, hands-on observation. In the picture, a younger Jasmyn is in a pink plaid pajama set, sitting in the middle of the couch with newborn Katarina in her arms. Paula and Kevin are in similar winter sleepwear, standing behind the two girls and leaning over the couch's back. In his Superman pajamas, eight-year-old Logan lays sprawled on the floor pretending to be asleep.

"How's Kat holding up?" Paula asks, hoping to hear no new developments since they spoke last night.

"She's still asleep. Everyone is resting since Patricia put the sleep spell on those dragons."

"Why can't she do that more often?"

"Casting the spell makes her weak. She can't do it indefinitely, I guess. They are going to lead the dragons out to the desert, where they can do less harm. Between her and Regina, they'll figure it out. They still need Kat."

"Need her for what? The spell didn't work."

"I don't know Paula." Kevin rubs his eyes. "I don't know."

After two decades of marriage, Paula usually discerns Kevin's stress through his tone, but this is a tone she isn't used to. He sounds dejected, as if he were giving up, and Paula isn't going to have it. *His mother's death, a family secret, dragons after his daughter, risking his daughter's life, and now another daughter missing; it's a lot for anyone to handle.* She takes the photo in her hands, feeling the presence of her daughters, raises her chin, and inhales a breath of inner strength. "Don't leave her," she says in a commanding tone as she adjusts her shirt so that it's straight and proper. With her index finger pointing down toward the ground, she says, "Whatever you do, don't leave her side. Logan and I will find Jaz. You take care of Kat." A small pause, a hard swallow, and a silent prayer later, Paula hangs up.

When Kevin rejoins the group in the conference room, Patricia approaches. "Kevin, this is Regina."

A tall, fair-skinned redhead wearing fitted jeans and a loose white tunic with rows of colorful beads bordering a scoop neckline, like an upside-down rainbow, walks toward Kevin with her arms open for an embrace. She is a striking contrast to Patricia's olive skin, jet-black hair, and conservative attire. "I am so sorry for your loss," Regina says wholeheartedly as she hugs him once more. "We'll fix this. I promise you."

The clanking of wooden and silver bangles on Regina's arms catches Patricia's attention. She pulls Regina aside and inspects her outfit, down to her tiny dreamcatcher earrings. "Navajo?" she asks, pointing at the charms with her index finger.

"Ojibwe," Regina says.

"I thought Armando was Navajo."

"That was Erik. Erik was Navajo. Armando's Chippewa ancestry goes way back."

"So he's the new influence in your life?"

Regina waves her hand as if she's clearing dust in the air. "No. I broke up with him last year, but I love the Chippewa culture. You can never bring too many good intentions into situations like this. We need all the help we can get."

Gustavo puts his hand on Kevin's shoulder and squeezes. "Is everyone alright at home?"

After a half-dozen rapid eye blinks, Kevin nods without saying a word. He can't even speak about Jasmyn's disappearance. His tears are barely contained, and his jaw muscles are in a constant state of compression. *Paula will find Jaz. She's fine. She has to be.* Kevin pushes through the knot in his throat and addresses Patricia. "What's the plan?"

Once everyone gathers around the conference table, Patricia explains what she has been doing for the last few hours. She took a small strand of hair from Katarina's head and cast a third-eye spell in a bowl of clear water to see if she could see the moment when the dragons were released. She wanted to make sure Katarina wasn't mistaken about the words she had recited from the *Book of Whispers*, or perhaps see if Katarina had accidentally cast another series of incantations that may have altered her ability to manipulate the dragons. The spell Patricia executed replayed parts of Katarina's life from the night Agatha died. She didn't see anything worth suspecting.

Patricia then remembered the family photo Gustavo showed her at the wake and slipped it from his suit jacket while he was sleeping. She cast a similar spell on everyone in the photo, in case they had something to do with Katarina since their grandmother passed away. Nothing in the water gave Patricia any more information.

"Then, I remembered that Jasmyn had destroyed the box. The box is indestructible by natural forces—only magic can destroy it." Patricia looks to Regina for confirmation. "I'm only guessing, but, somehow, Agatha gave both Katarina and Jasmyn her gifts."

"The Blood Rites Ritual explicitly states that a single female from your own bloodline inherits your gift," Regina says. "How could Agatha have given them both her powers? It's not possible."

Patricia shrugs her shoulders. "Evidently it is. How else can you explain the destruction of the box? Katarina didn't read any incantations that would have weakened the box's power. Also, when we were in the backyard, Jasmyn said she felt vibrations from me. But then, the explosions, the news, the military…everything happened so fast." Her slender fingers comb her silky black hair behind her head in one slow stroke. "That must be it."

"I thought it was odd that Agatha chose Katarina instead of Jasmyn." Regina places her index finger over her mouth and wraps her chin with her thumb. "Did you sense anything when you met her?"

"Not really. Although," Patricia snaps her fingers, "she did give me a strange look when she walked into the funeral parlor—a long stare, as if she was studying me. She must have sensed me."

A slow huff escapes Regina as she shakes her head in disbelief. "Agatha really made a mess of this, didn't she? Two half-witches, each with different powers and abilities. Together, they'd be a hell of a sorceress." Regina's eyes widen, and Patricia matches her look of surprise.

"That might be why the spell didn't work—they both have to perform it." Patricia rubs her hands together and paces around the room as the plan unfolds in her mind. "We have to get Jasmyn here so she and Katarina can read the spell together."

"That's going to be a problem." Kevin swallows before continuing. "Paula and Logan are out looking for Jaz right now. She didn't come home last night."

"I thought you said everyone was fine," Gustavo whispers.

Kevin bites down hard on his bottom lip, and his eyes become red.

"Jasmyn is safe," Patricia says. "In fact, she's on her way home right now. Call Paula and tell her and Logan to stay put."

Kevin pulls out his phone and begins dialing.

"Walter, can we get someone to pick Jasmyn up at the house and bring her here?"

"I'll see what I can do."

"Brian Santiago," Patricia snaps her fingers again as the name of the boy Patricia saw in the third-eye spell comes to her. "Tell Paula that Jasmyn is with Brian Santiago."

~ ~ ~

Brian hasn't thought much about Jasmyn McKeery since he last saw her eight years ago on the day her family moved up north. And now he finds her fast asleep in a white sedan parked at a 24-hour food mart. At first, he didn't recognize Jasmyn's wavy auburn hair, mostly because she used to wear a black cowboy hat whenever they played together in their connecting backyards. But now, as he approaches the car to get a better look, he sees his old childhood friend napping away, mouth agape, as if she has not a care in the world.

He taps on her window with his fingernail. She doesn't wake.

The slim pickings from the marketplace make a tumbling sound as he tosses his groceries to the back of his black SUV parked right next to Jasmyn's sedan. He was lucky to find what he did—a gallon of milk, a few bottles of water, sliced raisin bread, peanut butter, and a box of crackers. Panic has practically shut the city down. Aside from the occasional military aircraft flying by, Brian's neighborhood is pretty quiet, in an apocalyptic, abandoned-city sort of way.

"Jaz?" he says as he thumps his knuckle on the glass.

Jasmyn's eyes shoot open. She takes in a quick breath and raises her head, squinting at the face peering down on her. "Brian?"

"Are you alright?" His voice sounds muffled through the car's window.

As she wipes the corners of her eyes and mouth, Jasmyn sits up and takes inventory of her situation. While her mind whizzes away at concocting suitable excuses for her disheveled appearance, she steps out of the sedan and straightens her shirt. The second she glances at Brian's honey-gold eyes, she feels

116

embarrassed and vulnerable. She says nothing, lowering her gaze to the ground.

Brian doesn't wait for her answer and takes a step closer to her to wipe a dried tear streak from her cheek. He fears the answer to the question he's about to ask. "Jaz, where is your family?"

Brian sees Jasmyn's face contort with pain, and he instinctively pulls her in. He wraps his arms around her shoulders as if he's done it a million times before, without hesitation, without intentions. Jasmyn digs her head into his chest and releases every sob she's held in for the past few days. He strokes her hair and shushes her, and she cries more.

How could Nana have chosen Kat over me? Did she love me so little, so insignificantly? Did she think I was heartless? I had to be hard. I had to be cold. How could I give them affection if they never gave me any? Except hate...they show me how much they hate me. Their hate cuts me.

After a minute, Jasmyn steps out of Brian's embrace. "My family is fine," she says with a tight voice, wishing she was still being compressed by his arms. "My grandmother passed away a few days ago, but my family is fine."

A sigh of relief passes through Brian's lips. "I'm so sorry about your grandmother. I remember her. She used to read you that book, about the magic spells. You used to talk about them all the time."

Jasmyn nods with her eyes aimed at the ground, unable to look at him.

He brushes her hair back behind her ear and waits patiently for her to continue.

"I left them," she says, her throat feeling less constricted. She straightens her back and lifts her chin. "They wanted me to leave. They practically kicked me out, so I left them."

"In the middle of all this chaos?" He shakes his head. "I doubt that. Do they know you're here?"

"No. They probably don't care."

A smirk crosses Brian's face, and he rolls his eyes. "Please don't tell me you moved uptown and turned into one of those spoiled, dramatic high school girls from a clichéd movie."

"No. It's nothing like that." A warm sensation radiates from him toward Jasmyn. The stiffness in her neck and shoulders begins to melt. The achiness in her muscles dissolves. Her back relaxes, and her breathing normalizes as the blanket of serene vibrations covers her entire body. *What is this? What's happening to me?* A silly grin appears on Jasmyn's face as the warmth sinks in, grabbing hold of her tension and lifting it away from her body. *This is nice.*

Brian's heart flutters the instant he sees her smile. Casually, he takes a long, deep breath before asking in a tender voice, "Jaz, why were you crying?"

"It's a long story. You'll probably think I'm crazy when you hear it."

"Haven't you heard? There are dragons and man-eating monsters all over California. Whatever you tell me probably won't surprise me."

Jasmyn smiles again, demurely. "You want to bet?"

While eating a breakfast of crackers and peanut butter at Brian's apartment, accompanied by milk served in plastic cups, Jasmyn tells Brian the entire story. He listens intently, asks only a few questions, and accepts everything she says about the dragons and witches as fact. He doubts only the parts about her personal family drama and convinces her to let them know she's safe.

Her phone ran out of battery last night, so she dials her house number on Brian's cell phone. "The call's not going through."

His wooden kitchenette chair creaks when he leans forward to grab his cell phone. He tries a few numbers without success. "The cell phone towers must be flooded with calls." With a quick flip of his wrist, he stuffs his phone in his pants. "My truck has a full tank. We can be at your house in less than an hour."

Jasmyn lowers her eyes to the side.

"Jaz, you have to be with your family."

"They don't want me there."

"I don't believe that for a second."

"You don't know…"

Brian arches a single eyebrow, waiting for Jasmyn to finish her sentence. "Know what?"

With her arms and legs crossed, she shrugs her shoulders. "They just don't want me there."

The chair screeches along the hardwood floor when Brian slides it backwards to stand up. "We're going to your house." He grabs his backpack and fills it with a few water bottles and snacks. From a black plastic crate full of cords and wires, he yanks out a USB charger for Jasmyn's cellphone. "If, after you see your parents, you still want to leave, I'll take you wherever you want to go."

"You don't have to do that."

"Jaz, there are monsters out there. If it were my sister who was found by your brother, I know he would make sure she got home in one piece."

"You don't have any sisters." She says the corners of her lip curved upward.

"That's beside the point."

Pressing her lips to keep herself from smiling, Jasmyn recalls how bossy Brian used to be when he was younger. He would try to dictate all their pretend play, the details of their worlds, the personality and backstory of each alien that attacked

119

the Milky Way. When she would make up her own universe and take control of the armies defending the solar system against Brian's will, he would, in retaliation, play the villain and attack her planet. Eventually, at the end of every long sunny afternoon, they would wind up on the same side.

They were the best of friends, and Jasmyn was the first crush Brian ever had. When he was ten and Jasmyn was eight, on Valentine's Day, he swore he would marry her and buy her a big house with a big backyard so they could have all the dogs they would ever want. She had giggled and left him standing in the schoolyard when he made her that promise, and Brian didn't speak to her for a full week of school—a lifetime for a fifth-grader. Eventually, Jasmyn appeared at Brian's front door wearing a white football helmet—her space helmet—and told him they needed to defend the galaxy from the Neon Grimy Beasts from the planet Zorgowl. Without thinking too hard about it, Brian grabbed his own football helmet and followed Jasmyn to the backyard. All was forgiven.

It was no wonder why Jasmyn cried so much when she moved to San Francisco. On the day she moved, two years after Brian declared his love for her and was rejected, he made her promise they would never stop being friends. After sealing the deal with a pinky swear, Jasmyn watched Brian wave to her from the middle of the street until her car turned the corner, and he was out of her sight.

Now, as she watches him pack his backpack with concentration, looking around for things he might need, Jasmyn realizes the eyeglass-wearing, skinny boy from her childhood is a far cry from the young man she sees today. Immediately behind Brian she spots a giant poster with a prototypical 1950s flying saucer above the words "I want to believe." Jasmyn smiles and shakes her head. *Still the same old kid defending the universe.*

On his way from the kitchen to his bedroom, Brian walks around his small kitchenette table and right in front of Jasmyn. She stands and slides her seat in to give him room. The space is so small that when he gets close to her the same warm waves from earlier hit her dead on and make her feel weak in the knees. Her arms reach for the chair behind her for balance. When Brian finally passes her and heads to the bedroom, he takes the vibrations with him. Jasmyn sighs with relief, feeling as if she just received a deep-tissue massage. *I have to get a handle on this, whatever this is. Just breathe.*

In a mind-over-body effort to work through the fatigue, she takes a moment to scan Brian's studious apartment. Several pieces of computing equipment are hooked up to monitors and other machines of various shapes and sizes. Books on computer science, programming, and electrical engineering line the packed metal bookcase in his living room. On the round center table, an application to participate in a scholarship competition for Stanford lies open, partially filled out. She takes a seat on a leather rocking chair and picks up a photo of him and his family mounted on the side table. "Where are your parents?" Jasmyn asks, just now noticing that he lives in the one-bedroom apartment alone.

"They sold the house and bought a huge plot of land in Colombia. They couldn't wait to get out of here, them and their cousins. They all left." He walks back into the living room with his backpack in hand.

"So you don't have any family here?"

"Nope." He shrugs his shoulders as if it didn't matter to him. "I made the choice to stay. They wanted to leave. I didn't want my parents to stay here just for me, and I wouldn't have been happy in Colombia."

"Have you spoken to them recently?"

"Yesterday, once the news hit." He gestures toward the

television that is set on low volume, the news replaying scenes from last night. Completely unaware of the events of the past evening, Jasmyn is mesmerized by the news footage and grabs the remote to raise the volume. She hasn't heard any news since she left her home last night. She had driven in silence, allowing only her misery to guide her path onward. She kept recalling the knives piercing her skin, unable to shake the notion that it was her family's loathing of her that caused the sensation. When she remembered the way Logan commanded her to leave, she felt Logan's voice slice through her again, as if it was trying to cut through to her heart. That's when she realized she was feeling their emotions. She felt her family's hatred of her last night stabbing her, trying to break her, trying to kill her.

Now she sees her family on the news. "That's my mom closing the door on the reporter."

A portly man with a thin shadow of a beard, wearing a military uniform with dozens of medals pinned to his jacket, talks about the military history of the pilot. Another so-called expert on the supernatural speculates on the reason they were flying so close to the dragons, why the dragons are heading to a specific spot, and why only one of them is killing every human being in his path. "There are an estimated one hundred fifty thousand casualties, with the number continuing to grow as more calls come in."

Jasmyn gasps. *One hundred fifty thousand people are dead because of me.* Another video, taken from a helicopter, shows what's left of the Golden Gate Bridge up in flames, fire burning on the surface of the water and atop the buildings that lined the dragon's path. The helicopter cameraman jerks the camera around as the pilot climbs suddenly, avoiding a burst of fire from the black dragon. Jasmyn holds her breath until the cameraman comes back online and explains what just happened.

"That's Katarina, in the helicopter!" Jasmyn shouts just

before the news replays the footage of the black dragon breathing fire at the helicopter carrying her sister.

Brian watches the video and sees the horror in Jasmyn's eyes. He rummages through his closet, pulls out a long, black vinyl case, and slings it over his shoulder. He throws his backpack over his other arm. "Let's go before those dragons wake up."

14

THE MINIONS

"Where the hell are you?" Logan screams into the house phone in an unusually threatening tone. Paula sits down and releases the enormous breath she's been holding since she woke up, feeling relieved and, at the same time, infuriated at Jasmyn for waiting so long to call.

"We were on Junipero, but we had to get out at Hillsborough. The highway is demolished. We're trying to go around the lake, but the roads are packed. It took a while to find a payphone."

Logan covers the phone and speaks to everyone in his kitchen. "She's by San Andreas Lake. She's trying to cut through the park. The highways are jammed."

A military officer dressed in combat uniform addresses Logan. "We can pick her up by chopper. We just need her to go to an open area."

"Jaz, listen carefully. There are some military people here who need you. You have to go to a spot where they can pick you up in a helicopter."

"Military? Why are they coming for me?"

"Kat needs you. She can't stop the dragons alone. You have to help her."

"Me? How?"

"Patricia said the box you smashed could only have been destroyed by another sorceress, someone with power. She thinks Nana shared her magic between the two of you."

"But, I thought—"

"Jaz!" Logan takes a deep breath, wishing his sister would just listen without questioning every single sentence. "Kat needs you to help get those dragons under control. She can't do this without you."

The soldier takes the phone from Logan's hand and raises it to his square jaw. "Jasmyn, this is Sergeant Keppler from the Unites States Marines. Can you drive to San Andreas Lake?"

"We're not too far from there. Brian says he knows how to get to the south side of the lake. There's a clearing near a small beach."

"Good. We're on our way."

Logan takes back the phone and waits a few seconds until the soldiers leave the room. "Jaz?"

"Yeah."

"Don't ever disappear like that again. Do you hear me? Ever!"

"Okay," she says, blinking back tears, feeling the bittersweet sense of sibling love from her brother's scolding. "I'll see you soon."

Brian smirks after Jasmyn ends the call. "Still think your family hates you?"

A thick concrete ball lodges itself in her esophagus as she walks back to the truck, constricting her ability to agree or disagree, and Brian smiles victoriously.

As they drive north on the Junipero Serra Freeway, the sight of so many automobiles sitting bumper to bumper on the southbound side of the road with drivers and passengers standing outside their cars makes the hair on the back of Brian's neck spike outwards. The ground suddenly trembles, forcing Brian to pull over onto the shoulder.

"Another earthquake? Now? Really?" Jasmyn asks as she

gets out of the car.

It stops.

"I don't think it's an earthquake," Brian says as he steps onto the running board to get a view above the traffic behind him.

The ground shakes again and stops within seconds. Another rumble, then silence.

Screams, the squealing of tires, gunfire, and explosions emanate from the road behind them. "Get in!" Brian shouts. In the rearview mirror, he sees cars being tossed into the air behind a frantic mob of people running in his direction. He floors the accelerator and heads for the lake.

Jasmyn grips the dashboard and side door handle as they speed down the freeway, veering around trucks that have jumped the divider and are now heading north. The truck jerks to the right as Brian exits to take the freeway underpass to enter the park. After a minute on the park's paved road, he turns onto a dirt road barely wide enough for his truck that leads right into a clearing of trees. He skids the car to a stop on the wild grass, turns off the engine, and heads to the back of his truck to pull out his two semi-automatics from the black vinyl bag. The clip snaps into place when he loads one of the rifles, just before handing it to Jasmyn.

Jasmyn's heart is already racing. "Where'd you get these?"

"My cousin's an ex-Marine. He used to take me to a shooting range every few months." He notices how comfortably Jasmyn is holding the weapon. "Have you ever fired a gun?"

Jasmyn looks down at her firearm. "No. But it can't be too hard, right? Line up the crosshairs and shoot?"

"Right. Watch the kickback. Make sure your feet are planted firmly when you fire. Hold it up like this, against your shoulder. Those monsters, they're not invincible like the dragons. They can be killed, so aim for the head."

Jasmyn nods and copies Brian's stance, aiming the barrel at bushes along the clearing. She presses the trigger and the power of the semi-automatic weapon pushes her back a few paces. Though she stumbles, she doesn't fall.

"I got it," she says to Brian once she regains her composure.

They jump over a short concrete divider and cross a bicycle path to get to the beach. With his right hand over his eyebrows, trying to block out the sun, Brian searches for military helicopters coming from the north. Jasmyn walks around the small beach in search of firm ground along the border. "This is the only beach on the south side of the lake?"

"The only one I know of."

A breeze ruffles the leaves in the towering trees and surrounds them with a shushing noise. The scent of natural forestry gives Jasmyn a sense of being hidden in the woods, hoping nature will protect them, somehow. *Think good thoughts, simple thoughts, positive thoughts about the future. What was going on before all this happened? Oh yeah...graduation, going to Berkeley, prom. Maybe I'll ask Brian to the prom. Prom? Really? Who the hell cares about prom? Concentrate! Kill the monsters. Help Kat.*

Commotion in the distance catches their attention, but nothing seems to be moving in their direction. Jasmyn inches backwards toward the lake's edge, stepping over jagged rocks jutting up and out from the ground. The ground softens as she gets closer to the water. Her heel sinks downward, deeper, and jerks her balance for a split second before she steadies herself. An idea fills her head. "Can they swim?"

As last night's news footage replays in Brian head, he widens his eyes. "A lot of them drowned in the bay. They're disproportionate. Might be hard for them to keep afloat."

Jasmyn raises her eyebrows. "Maybe they're just bad swimmers."

"Maybe."

At the same exact moment, they both spot a canoe turned upside-down along the shoreline just twenty feet away with the words "I WILL SURVIVE!" spray-painted in thick, black letters along the boat's white bottom. Jasmyn can't help but huff at the coincidence, looking at Brian, who also can't hold back a thankful grin. They dash to the canoe.

With their guns ready at their feet, they row the canoe away from the shore. As they drift out toward the middle of the lake, they see dark gray smoke rising from the road where Brian made the turn, sending an ominous message to anyone who would notice.

A single Canadian goose rises from behind the spread of trees at the beach and passes over and across the lake. Three more follow its trail. Soon, a symphony of squawks and honks emanate from the forest and dozens of birds of various sizes jump into flight.

"Keep rowing!" Brian shouts to Jasmyn as more birds fly overhead.

Like a beacon of hope, the rhythmic beat of helicopter blades approaches from the north side of the lake. The thumping sound catches the attention of the monsters wreaking havoc along the freeway. They cut through the trees, swinging and jumping across large tree branches, thrusting their bodies over boulders and bushes toward the giant metallic machine floating in the sky. When they reach the clearing, they head straight for the humans in the middle of the lake.

Machine guns fire from the helicopter down toward the creatures, killing them and creating a pile of carcasses blocking the path to the shore. More monsters appear, and more bullets are fired.

One beast grabs another by its ankles, spins in a circle and tosses it toward the helicopter, coming close to the chopper's blades. When it falls into the lake, it sinks straight down to the lake's bed like an anchor. One after another, monsters are shot-putted toward the aircraft, each toss coming dangerously close to the canoe. The pilot launches a missile toward shoreline, sending the monsters exploding into the air, creating a shockwave that causes large ripples in the water and forces the canoe to totter at drastic angles. Splashing water and dirt falling from the sky coat Jasmyn and Brian as they hold onto the edges of the canoe, trying to keep it balanced.

A second helicopter appears and takes on the task of killing the beasts as the first helicopter approaches the canoe. A soldier hanging onto a rope ladder descends toward Brian and Jasmyn to help them climb up to the chopper. Just as Jasmyn is halfway up the rope, a monster carcass hits the back corner of the canoe and flips it over, throwing Brian and the soldier into the lake. Once Jasmyn climbs into the helicopter cabin, the pilot once again lowers the helicopter closer to the lake's surface to lift Brian and the other soldier out of the water. With the cable finally in his hand, the soldier in the water hooks Brian to the rope ladder with a karabiner.

The instant Brian and the soldier are lifted out of the water another monster carcass flies past the spray of bullets and knocks them into a long swing. Brian is hooked onto the rope, but the soldier is not. The soldier loses his grip and goes flying into the lake, close to the beach. The monsters take action. They lob everything at the human in the water—body parts, rocks, each other, and soon the soldier is dragged under. He does not emerge.

"Go, go, go!" the soldier in the cabin yells at the pilot as he pulls Brian up on the cord while the helicopter ascends away from the lake.

"The kids are with us," the soldier shouts into the microphone attached to his helmet. "We have a man down."

A sickening feeling fills Jasmyn's stomach as she stares at the monsters piling on top of each other like hungry ants rushing over a piece of abandoned fruit. The beasts continue to propel pieces of their dead toward the helicopter, aiming at them with fury. Once the lake disappears in the distance, Jasmyn leans against Brian's shoulder and takes long, deep breaths to suppress her sense of guilt. When Brian wraps his arm around her, tears instantly flow down her cheeks. She presses her lips tight to keep from sobbing. *That soldier is dead because of me. Thousands of people are dead because of me. I did this. I destroyed that box.*

Brian holds her tighter, his eyes turning red as he struggles with his own mixed emotions. He asks the soldier seated in front of him for the name of the soldier who died saving his life—a name he will never forget.

They ride in silence for a few more minutes before a soldier passes Brian a tablet device bound in a thick plastic case. "My commanding officer said you had to take a look at this."

"This is Nana's *Book of Whispers*," Jasmyn says. "What am I supposed to do with it?"

"Those were my orders, ma'am."

"Can she speak to your commanding officer?" Brian asks.

The soldier hands Jasmyn a headset with a speakerphone attached to the side. When she puts it on, a deep, raspy voice speaks to her. "Jasmyn, this is Sergeant Keppler again. I'm about to connect you with your family at NAS Fallon. Stand by."

Once Patricia and Regina are on the line, they explain what they believe will need to happen to stop the dragons. Jasmyn pushes her guilt aside so she can listen carefully to their explanation.

"That's all we have to do?" Jasmyn asks. "What if it doesn't work?"

"Then we'll have to think of something else."

"Okay." Jasmyn nods. "So where's the spell?"

Regina furrows her eyebrows. "It's in the image. Can't you read it?"

"No."

Regina and Patricia roll their eyes. "We'll send you a translation."

"Shit," Kevin says as he watches the news, catching Patricia and Regina's attention. "The dragons are awake."

15

BROTHERHOOD

The morning sun stings Oxerion's and Baronyx's eyes. The two dragons lift their weary three-hundred-ton bodies from the ground, grunting with each crackle of joint and cartilage, their muscles straining against the spell that is finally wearing off. They are both confused as to why a thin, wiry blanket has been placed upon them.

"Brothers! Are you well?" Pterones calls out in a roar. "The sorceress did not touch me."

Baronyx senses Pterones nearby. "Don't kill anything. Don't give humans more reason to attack us," he begs.

"Your child witch tried casting an entrapment spell on you, regardless of your pleas. Does that not infuriate you?" Oxerion growls.

"It does not overshadow what I know to be right."

Smoke emanates from Oxerion's nostrils. "Do you not see she is trying to put you under her spell? She wants you to believe her, trust her, so she can enslave you." Oxerion notices the sky's bright blue color. "So much time has passed—she must have put us to sleep. You, Baronyx, are to blame if that witch entraps us again. We must stop her at once!"

"Instead, Brother, perhaps we should try to talk with Katarina. She seems willing to listen to Baronyx," Pterones says, sitting on a grassy hill with his head hung low as his minions pick at dry patches and pull on low-hung leaves with boredom.

"You see?" Baronyx stretches his wings, "Pterones can

read my thoughts as well. He can see that I speak the truth. Young Katarina is led by those who want us dead because of the destruction you have created. You brought this upon us three centuries ago, and you bring it again."

Baronyx pulls along the muscles of his back to extend his wings to their full length, standing on his hind legs and raising his head to tower over Oxerion's beaten stance, casting a shadow so ominous that Oxerion takes notice. As if made of spider silk instead of military-grade mesh, the netting snaps around both dragons. Baronyx's show of strength ends when Oxerion rises to his feet and releases a thunderous roar. News helicopters hovering far above the scene capture the frightening moment of absolute power. The military has no control over ancient mammoths.

Oxerion's large black wings cast a shadow so grand that it engulfs Baronyx's frame and three abandoned jetliners. "You think I need you or Pterones to kill that child witch?" He flaps his wings in what looks like slow motion, lifts his body sluggishly off the ground and heads toward the midmorning sun. Baronyx is soon in the air following the magnetic pull leading straight to Katarina.

In the air heading inland, Oxerion encounters a helicopter with a magical being inside and flaps his enormous wings harder. Baronyx also senses something supernatural on board, with a pull similar to Katarina's. "Oxerion will kill you! Get out of his way!" Baronyx roars, nearly shaking the helicopter side to side, hoping the passenger inside can understand him as Katarina did. The pilot regains control of the helicopter and begins picking up speed.

The pleading screams in Jasmyn's head sounds as if it's coming from somewhere within the helicopter cabin. She looks out the side window and spots the black and red dragons flying behind them.

Baronyx swears he sees Agatha looking out the window

of the helicopter. He concentrates as he did with Katarina and attempts to communicate with her. Tender moments between the red dragon and the witch called Finna appear in Jasmyn's mind. She sees the dragon's true intentions through scenes from the past few days in which he and his minions avoid human casualties. He apologizes for the damage his brothers have caused. His agony, his repentance, and his fear for her life provoke a dull pressure in her body. And just like Jasmyn felt her brother's stabbing anger last night and Brian's relaxing attraction earlier, she physically feels Baronyx's disquieted anxiety like a thousand tiny spoons pressing against her skin.

The connection, the bond between his brother and the witch that has formed in the past few seconds burns Oxerion to the core. He inhales an ocean of air into his cavernous lungs and releases a breath of fire that almost reaches the helicopter. "You want to see pain, witch. I will show you pain," Oxerion roars.

Through his own mental connection, Oxerion shows Jasmyn his detestation for humans, his animosity toward Finna and the witches, and his vengeful desire to eliminate the world of both beings. Repulsive images of his triumphant moments during the last battle reel in her mind. He burns witches to ashes, snaps the backs of dozens of humans in his snout, and tortures his brethren in secret when they don't follow his orders.

Jasmyn hunches over in her seat, inhales deeply, and blows out bursts of breath to control Oxerion's hatred jabbing her muscles.

"Breathe, Jaz. Breathe." Brian shouts.

"They are in my head!" Even in her thoughts, Oxerion and Baronyx battle for control.

With a sudden dive toward the earth, Oxerion distracts Baronyx's hold on Jasmyn's thoughts and concocts an image of a sweet, smiling, doe-eyed Katarina standing on the summit of a mountain. As the ocean's breeze blows her hair back away from her face, Oxerion snatches her up in his mouth and slams his jaws shut, drowning out her frightful screams. He chews, swallows, and chuckles.

"No!" Jasmyn wails. She sits upright and presses her head back against her headrest. Her fingers grip the bottom of her seat so hard her knuckles turn white.

A rumble shakes the helicopter as Oxerion roars once more. "You are no match for us, child."

Jasmyn screams in agony as the image replays itself in her mind, as if she were watching a real event. The breaking of her heart drowns out all the physical pain inflicted upon her.

At that moment, Baronyx puts all his energy into his wings and attacks Oxerion from behind. Pterones catches up to his brothers and flies in front of Oxerion to block his way, making sure the helicopter escapes safely. The three beasts fight in midair, shooting bursts of fire in all directions, pushing away clouds and smoke with their monumental wings. With the helicopter at full speed, the dragons disappear into the morning sky. Jasmyn cries softly as the pain subsides. She grimaces at the merciless visions.

"Jasmyn," Patricia says over the headphones, having heard everything that transpired. "What happened to you?"

Between shaky breaths, Jasmyn tries to explain. "The dragons…I heard them…their thoughts. I saw visions…" Jasmyn begins sobbing. Her voice shrieks. "Kat…she was…"

Patricia shouts over the phone. "Katarina is fine. She's here with us. Don't listen to them. They can get inside your head and make you see things that aren't real. Don't trust anything they say. Just get here as soon as you can. Regina and I will be able to hold them off until you and Katarina can fix this."

"But…Baronyx and the other dragon are fighting off Oxerion. They are helping us get away."

"Damn it!" With the phone down at her side, Patricia curses under her breath. "Baronyx connected with her too," she says, practically spitting the words out.

"He was Finna's favorite, and Agatha always felt guilty for entrapping him," Regina says. "He was as much a victim of Oxerion's uprising as any one of us."

"Are you saying we should trust him?" Patricia asks in an accusatory tone.

"No." Regina pauses. "We can use this to our advantage. We can use his trust in the girls to lure Baronyx and his brothers in."

"No!" Katarina shouts with her hands in fists at her side. "He's kind and gentle."

"You don't know what you're dealing with here, Katarina," Patricia says sharply. "These monsters are capable of destroying cities and killing hundreds of thousands of people. They will destroy the entire west coast before moving on to the rest of the country."

"Not him!"

With a forceful nudge, Regina pulls Patricia back and speaks to Katarina in a gentler tone. "Katarina, they are brothers. They will fight for each other's survival."

"Not Baronyx. He knew what I was trying to do." Katarina's eyes begin to water. "He knew I was going to cast the spell on him, and he still let me. He knows we have to trap them, and he didn't fight back. He's good."

"The dragons have a history of deception and destruction. We trusted them once, and that was costly. We lost everyone..." Patricia pauses before her voice matches the pain of her recollection. She swallows before continuing in a flat tone. "We cannot trust them again. We have to banish them all."

Katarina rushes to her father's arms looking for a

consoling embrace, the kind only a father can give. With his daughter's face buried in his shoulder, Kevin shushes in her ear and rocks on his feet. "Look at me, Kat." Katarina pulls back just enough to look up past the tears in her eyes.

"The most important thing in the world is family. You, Jaz, Logan, and your mother are everything to me. Anything that threatens our family has to be stopped. Do you understand?"

She nods, wiping her tears.

"Then you have to trap the dragons. You have to stop all of them to stop the bad one. I know it's not fair, but there is nothing else we can do. We have to take care of our family first."

Sniffling, Katarina rests her head on her father's shoulder. Her face softens as the last of her remorseful tears stream down her cheeks.

~ ~ ~

Though no manmade weaponry or supernatural sorcery can breach the dragons' mystical shield, they were created with one weakness: They are capable of ripping each other apart. Finna did not do this intentionally when she gave the dragons life; however, magic has a way of maintaining its own natural balance. Because of this weakness, Baronyx's sharp teeth and claws penetrate the folds of Oxerion's wings. He tears gaping holes into the flesh, causing the gargantuan beast to plummet to the earth without control.

Oxerion crashes into a low, rolling mountain range causing a quake that travels for miles. Although Baronyx succeeds in keeping his brother from reaching Jasmyn's helicopter, he knows this is only a setback. He has to think of a way to change his brother's mind.

"Oxerion, please, let's stop fighting." Baronyx hovers

next to Pterones. "The world is large, and there are distant lands that are uninhabitable by humans. We can live there peacefully without worry, without causing any more destruction."

Oxerion stretches his wings to examine the torn flesh, a permanent mark of his brother's betrayal. Oxerion mourns his loss; he will never be able to take to the skies again. His resentment reaches its boiling point. A line has been crossed. However selfish his nature, Oxerion's desire was for true independence. Now any purity left in him transforms into blind, vengeful rage.

Red flames appear in Oxerion's eyes. He roars, "A brother would not render his brother flightless and aid those who are trying to kill him. Neither you nor Pterones are my brothers. We are no longer in alliance."

Flattening shrubs with each step, Oxerion walks down the mountainside following the pull. Baronyx and Pterones follow in the air, watching him trudge his way eastward toward Katarina.

The bushes crackle when Pterones lands in front of Oxerion, bringing him to a complete stop. He is loyal to both brothers; he doesn't want to betray Oxerion any more than let Baronyx down. He loves his brothers; they are the only thing he can call his own. However dysfunctional they are, Oxerion and Baronyx are his family.

"Brother, please listen to Baronyx," Pterones pleads. "The young witches seem open to listening to him, considering our side. If we can find a way to—"

With fire still burning in his eyes, Oxerion inhales deeply and stands tall over Pterones, roaring louder than ever before. "Do not address me as your brother, Pterones. You did nothing as Baronyx tore my wings apart. You allowed the witch to escape, to live another day to plot our demise. You and Baronyx helped my enemy. We are not brothers. We are not family!" Oxerion lunges at Pterones and sinks his jagged teeth into Pterones' neck, cutting the flow of blood from his body and tearing out a giant chunk of flesh from his throat. Pterones' thunderous wail lasts only a few seconds before his body crashes down the side of the steep hill.

The pain and agony Pterones feels as the life is ripped out of his body is also Baronyx's to bear. He feels Oxerion's teeth slice through Pterones' thick skin, tear the strands of muscle along his neck, pierce his pumping arteries, and crush the bones trailing up his spine. Centuries of his younger brother's memories flash before his eyes, of proud moments between younger dragons during simpler times. As Pterones' life force disintegrates into nothingness, Baronyx roars up to the skies. His younger brother no longer exists.

With his brother's blood still dripping down the sides of his snout and chest, Oxerion turns to Baronyx and growls. "You think Finna created us to live in peace and harmony with the world? These puny humans and their machines cannot stop us. We are invincible. Finna created us so that she could rule the world. I am merely finishing what she started."

Baronyx aches for his younger brother, the smallest of the three, and the most loyal of all the Gregorn Dragons ever created. He cries out, "Finna loved us. She created us with hearts and minds so we wouldn't act like vicious, mindless animals."

"Use the mind she gave you. Why would a supernatural being create invincible, menacing, fire-breathing beasts if not to use them to conquer the world? You don't want to believe your mother was a selfish witch, but that is exactly what she was. We were a tool." Oxerion spits out blood from his mouth.

His head hanging lower, Baronyx stares at his dead brother. "We were their protectors. We defended them against the Foreman Clan, against the unsuspecting humans trying to conquer the Isle of Enid. We were made to defend them. If she knew you would turn out this way, she would never have created you."

He releases another painful roar, though it is softer, as he begins to cope with his loss. Not only has Baronyx lost Pterones, but he has also lost Oxerion. His wings slump over his body as if they were heavy cloaks draped across his back instead of instruments of flight. The bare truth of the matter becomes clear in his mind: He has to kill Oxerion to save Finna's bloodline and the entire human race. He is alone, with no sibling dragons, and he may soon suffer the fate of being the only Gregorn Dragon left on the planet.

Oxerion hears Baronyx's tormenting thoughts and feels emboldened in his position. "The paths of the great are taken alone, without brothers, without weaknesses, and without regrets. I will leave you to mourn your brother, but know that I will kill those witches. And if you stand in my way, I will kill you as well."

16

A BRIEF REUNION

The conference door slams open, peeling everyone away from the flat screen television with live news coverage of the black dragon crossing Mount Siegel. A soldier in military uniform walks over to Walter. "The chopper with your family has arrived. They're heading over."

"Did you see that?" Kevin asks Patricia as the battle replays on the screen. "He killed the smaller dragon. Why?"

"I don't know," Patricia says softly. "It doesn't make sense. Why would he kill Pterones and not Baronyx? He didn't strike him down. He just walked away."

"They are divided," Regina says, lowering her head to think about next steps. "Maybe we can get Katarina close enough to—"

"No," Kevin says. "I don't want her going anywhere near those things."

"You don't get it, Kevin," says Patricia. "They are pulled by her very presence. Her magic draws them. We have to confront them."

"Just keep putting them under that sleep spell. That worked for almost nine hours."

Exasperated, Patricia shakes her head and walks away.

"Kevin," Regina says, "Controlling spells are dark in nature. Patricia was exhausted from that one cast not only because of the enormity of the physical strain but also because she fought off the darkness that tempted her. It's very easy for any of us to

fall prey to dark magic; the warm feeling of power, it's…it's…"
Regina's eyelids flutter, "intoxicating. If she—or any of us—uses it too often, we may lose ourselves."

"You're asking me to risk my daughter's life. Again."

Patricia steps toward Kevin and says in a harsh tone, "We are going to risk both of your daughters." She narrows her eyes. "Don't forget about Jasmyn. She and Katarina are in the same boat."

With a hand pulling on Patricia's arm, Regina eases her reproach. The bangles on her wrists clank together as she interlocks her fingers into a prayer fold. "Your daughters' lives will always be at risk if we don't stop these dragons."

Logan and Paula rush into the room and embrace Katarina and Kevin. The happy reunion is cut short once Patricia explains the details of their plan. "Regina and I will create a diversion on the ground to keep the dragons distracted while Katarina and Jasmyn read the spell. You're going to do it from the helicopter, like before, with Walter at the controls."

"Both of them have to go up?" Paula asks, looking back at Kevin who holds Katarina's hand tightly in his. "What if it doesn't work again? What's the plan then?"

The uncertainty in their faces is clear; neither Patricia nor Regina has a backup plan.

"Then we will have to stall them until we come up with another solution. The desert is safest, in terms of reducing human casualties. And if we can't find any other way, we might have to resort to black magic. That would be our last option."

The worrisome but determined look in Patricia's eyes unnerves Regina. With reluctance, Regina nods. If one of them has to turn dark in order to entrap the dragons, the other will be there to eliminate the darkness by ending the life of her sister witch. Patricia will sacrifice herself, and Regina will have to destroy her.

Pacing, with his arms crossed, Logan sighs. "What was Nana thinking? Kat's only eight, and Jaz...none of this would've happened if she just let the magic die with her."

"No," Katarina says. She releases her father's tight grip and walks toward her brother. "This is who Nana was. It's as if she hasn't died. It's as if she's a part of me now. I can feel it. It's as if she's alive inside of me." She stares down at her hands for a second before looking back up at Logan with her nose scrunched. "Does that make sense?"

With his little sister's innocent gaze looking up at him, Logan's face softens and he offers her a smile. Enamored, he lowers his head to her eye level. "It makes total sense, but I still wish her magic died with her."

A commotion in the hallway catches everyone's attention, and the conference room becomes quiet as they hear a rush of footsteps.

"Which door?" Jasmyn asks.

A soldier points down the hallway. "The last door to the right."

"Kat!" Jasmyn shouts once her feet pick up the pace. "Kat!"

"Jaz!" Katarina shouts back..

Although her little sister is only a few feet away, Jasmyn dashes toward Katarina as fast as her feet allow. She picks her up and gives her the most compressed hug she has ever given her in her entire life. Katarina embraces her older sister, causing a hum that massages Jasmyn's shoulders and back and relaxes the tension in her stomach. Jasmyn's fear and resentment rises up and away, leaving her with the simple pleasure of loving her little sister.

"I am so, so sorry Kat," Jasmyn wipes the tears from her face. "I will never let anything happen to you. I swear it."

"You promise?"

"I swear, with my soul."

Jasmyn squeezes her arms tighter, ignoring everyone else in the room, and soon feels her knees weaken. Another blanket of warmth cocoons her when Logan embraces the two sisters kneeling on the floor. Even more tension-releasing vibrations enwrap her muscles once her parents complete the group hug. Jasmyn's eyelids get heavy as the pure emotions from her family calms her into a sleepy state. She slinks down to the ground, unconscious, but Logan grabs hold of her wrists before her head hits the floor. He carries her to a chair and slaps her with a gentle backhand.

"Don't worry," Patricia says with the corner of her lips in a slight upward turn. "I remember seeing this happen with Agatha once she joined the coven. It took her a while to get it right. She had a hard time controlling her ability as well."

"What ability?" Logan says. "She passed out!"

Blinking awake, Jasmyn sits up tall in her chair. "How long was I asleep?"

"Just for a few seconds." Patricia moves closer. "How do you feel?"

"Like I just had a full body massage."

"You have an empathic sense. You can physically feel other people's emotions and intentions. Everyone has some level of empathy that helps us read a person's true motives, that's part of what makes us human, but this extra sense is one of Agatha's gifts. She called it a curse at first, but then she learned to control it. Some emotions hurt, like you are being attacked, and some feel warm and fuzzy. Your family just showered you with love and you absorbed their emotions. It relaxed you to the point of unconsciousness."

"Nana had this? She could tell how we truly felt?"

Patricia nods and lifts her eyebrows.

Jasmyn swallows hard, suddenly remembering all the times she hid her emotions, held everything in, and kept a straight face even when she felt alone, betrayed, and unwanted. *All this time, Nana knew how I felt.* And just as quickly, an even shadier, more excruciating truth arises. Jasmyn recalls the amount of time she wasted feeling jealousy and bitterness toward her little sister and her parents. All this time she thought her negative feelings were her own dark secrets that only she had the burden of knowing. She was wrong. Her grandmother knew everything.

"That's a cool gift," Regina says, breaking Jasmyn's contemplation. "I've always liked that one."

"Will I have that gift?" Katarina asks, sitting on Jasmyn's lap. She looks up at Regina and Patricia with wide, honest eyes.

"I'm not sure, sweetheart," Regina says. "I don't know what you two are capable of doing." A sigh escapes Regina as she smiles at the beautiful image of the two sister witches. Agatha's life, her future, her soul sits right in front of her in these two girls. As for Patricia, she wrinkles her forehead, wondering how and why Agatha split her magic between them.

Brushing a loose strand of hair behind her sister's ear, Jasmyn smiles. "If I can share this gift with you, I will."

"Promise?" Katarina raises her right pinky and Jasmyn interlocks it with hers.

"Promise."

A million tiny tingling vibrations come from the far end of the room and tickle Jasmyn at her side. She lifts her eyes to follow the stream and spots Brian staring at her. He turns away, smiling, and walks toward the back of the room taking the wave of tiny vibrations with him.

~ ~ ~

When Walter announces the helicopter is ready, Logan steps up. "I want to go too."

"Sorry kid, there's no more room."

Kevin walks over to Logan and whispers. "You have to stay with Mom; I don't want to leave her alone. We'll be back soon enough."

With an unexpected ache in his chest, Logan turns away, disappointed. His father puts one hand on his shoulder, presses tightly, and frowns. Paula is already in tears, but she keeps her sobs in as she reassures Katarina that nothing will happen to her as long as Jasmyn, Dad, and Uncle Gustavo are with her.

"I'll be right next to you, okay?" Jasmyn says as she holds Katarina's trembling hands, listening to her heart beat through her tiny frame. "You are a strong little girl, the strongest I've ever known. You're stronger than I ever was. You can do this. That's why Nana chose you."

Katarina nods and takes a deep breath. "I think she chose both of us."

The smile between the two sisters is one of soldiers in the same war, the solid knowing smile of two people sharing a secret. For the first time in both their lives, Jasmyn and Katarina understand each other. The new connection between the two sisters is an unbreakable bond, that of sister witches about to go into battle.

Jasmyn walks over to Brian, who has been standing under the flat screen monitor, away from the family reconciliation. His smirk is a bit smug. "I'm not one to say 'I told you so,' but…"

"Then don't say it." Jasmyn leans her shoulder into his chest while looking at the floor. "Thank you," she whispers.

As foreboding images flash in his mind, Brian wraps his

146

arms around her shoulders and takes an unsteady breath. He swallows hard, forcing the unwelcomed visions away and replacing them with happier ones. "You can thank me later, when all this is over."

Fighting against the gentle, warm, inviting vibrations coming from Brian's direction, Jasmyn pulls herself back and away. When she looks up into his light hazel eyes, she sees his worry and attempts a smile. "I will."

"Okay," Patricia says, interrupting their moment, "Remember, Katarina reads the spell and then Jasmyn opens and closes the box. We'll switch the roles if it doesn't work. Got it?"

Jasmyn nods confidently.

"Let's go before the dragon gets any closer," Walter says, signaling the girls to say goodbye to their mother.

As they begin filing into the hallway, Gustavo walks over to Patricia, entering her personal space, and whispers, "Promise me you will do everything in your power to bring the girls back alive, even if you have to sacrifice us."

His pained eyes burn a hole through Patricia's wall and straight into her heart. She can see herself holding him, loving him, consoling him, living her life with him. Although she has been daydreaming about Gustavo for the past twenty-four hours, and trying to avoid his sideways glances, she knows the life of these two little girls is worth more to him than a relationship with an immortal doomed from the start. "I promise," she whispers.

Patricia doesn't remember when Gustavo reached for her hand, but when he releases it, she feels a loss. As she turns to follow a soldier down the hallway, a solitary tear forms in her right eye, and she quickly wipes it away before reaching Regina, who witnessed the interaction from down the corridor.

"He's a handsome one," Regina says playfully. "Looks like you two are hitting it off. Agatha would have been happy about that."

"Nothing's going to happen between us," she replies.

They push past the security doors and follow the soldier to a large black Humvee with the engine roaring.

"Why not? He seems totally into you, though I don't know why with your over-the-top hard-to-get attitude. And he practically turns you into putty."

"Exactly," Patricia replies without looking. "I don't want to be weak. I'm not interested in a relationship."

After Patricia climbs into the backseat and slides over, Regina looks back toward the building. "Maybe I'll give him a shot. He's gorgeous. Have you seen his body?"

Patricia sighs and presses her lips together into a thin line.

"The things I could do with a man like that…a firefighter no less. Hmmm."

"Stop it."

Desert dust fills the air as the Humvee starts rolling. The rumbling sound of gravel beneath the wheels reminds Patricia of the crumbling mountainside during the final battle with the dragons. She concentrates on elemental spells she hasn't used in centuries, and takes notice of the physical elements available to her in the surrounding environment. On the Isle of Enid, surrounded by water, aquatic elemental spells were more efficient than those that used rock or air. It was quicker to transform water to ice than to compress blocks of air into a solid weapon. Rock and dirt, already solidified, were readily available, but the side effect was instability in the land from which it was pulled. *There won't be any landslides here in the desert, though we need to watch for cracks in the earth.* She glances upwards. *Those clouds don't have enough moisture to pull water.* She looks to Regina who is taking off her bracelets and necklaces and storing her trinkets in her pockets. *Regina's never been in a battle. She's never had to use her powers in this way. This is going to be rough.*

The soldier notifies them the dragons are twenty minutes away.

"Since you're not interested in Gustavo, you won't mind if I make a move, right?" Regina asks playfully.

"I never said I didn't like him. I...just..."

"What? Spit it out already."

"He wants children. I saw it in his aura."

"So? It comes with the territory."

"I can't have children, Regina. I can't pass on this curse to them."

"It's a gift, Patricia, not a curse."

"Look what our *gift* has done to the world, to his family."

"Our gift didn't do this. Agatha did this. It was her irresponsibility that caused this chaos. When you have children-"

"If!"

Regina laughs. "Fine. *If* you have children, you will prepare them for everything. This would never happen."

Patricia shakes her head. "If I have children, I wouldn't want them to have any of this. I would probably let my gift die with me." She rolls her eyes. "I sound just like Agatha."

A triumphant smile crosses Regina's face. "Ah, as it is, the stone cold witch has a warm heart after all, talking about marriage, children. What did my mother used to say? 'And all is right and balanced with the world, as it always is in the world of magic.'"

"My mother used to say the same thing."

"Did she now? Maybe one day you'll say it to your own children." A quick succession of images from Katarina's memories fill Patricia's head, and she sees Agatha saying those same words to her granddaughter after reading stories from the *Book of Whispers*. She feels Agatha's warmth, her sincerity as she told the stories with rich detail and lively descriptions. She shakes the memory out of her mind and decides not to mention it to Regina for fear the gloating she knows will follow.

"I saw her," Patricia says. "I saw Agatha's old, wasted body in the coffin. I don't want to die that way."

"Who's talking about dying? I'm talking about living, loving, about being loved. Children, grandchildren, life, death…it's all messy, but it only makes sense if we have love in our lives."

"You're one to talk about love. You date men as a sport."

"Hey! If I found The One, I wouldn't hesitate. Besides, there's no love quite like a child's love. I'm sure I'll eventually pick a suitor and have a baby if I can't find my own Elliot. I mean, look at Agatha's family. They loved her unconditionally. I'm jealous of what she had, of the legacy she left behind."

Patricia rolls her eyes and huffs through a crooked smile.

"Okay, maybe not this band of misfit witches, but you know what I mean. Her life lives on in them, and in their children, and in their children's children. Through them, she's still immortal."

The next fifteen minutes pass quickly as Patricia's mind flips from one side to the other, deciding between allowing herself to care about Gustavo and ending it before anything can begin. Neither side has a chance to win as the horizon brings up the ominous sight of a large, black, fuming dragon.

"He's alone." Regina glances at Patricia. "Where is Baronyx?"

"Dead, I hope."

17

WITHOUT WINGS

The cadence of the helicopter blades on Walter's chopper causes the witches to drift off into their own thoughts. Jasmyn convinces herself that thinking about Berkeley, about the near future, is a sign that things will turn out alright. *I wonder if there's still a Berkeley to go to. I wonder how much damage the dragons have done, how much of a mess I'm responsible for. It seems so meaningless now, college, studying. Maybe I won't go in the fall. Maybe I'll stay home with Kat for a while. Yeah...I'll stay home for a long while.*

With her older sister's arm wrapped around her shoulders, Katarina feels a sense of confidence. She imagines playing in her backyard under a blanket of shimmering stars, running around the fresh grass, barefoot, with Jinx chasing her feet. In her hopeful vision, Jasmyn watches the whole spectacle and eventually joins the fruitless chase around their yard. Simple everyday pleasure is what Katarina desires, with her sister in her life. *But first, I have to do this. I can do this.*

"There's the black dragon," Walter brings the sisters back to the task at hand. "He's alone. I don't see the other."

With the heavy steps of a disgruntled beast, Oxerion hauls his primeval body across the desert. Although several helicopters are hovering over Oxerion, as they have been for the past few hours, he pays no mind to them. He marches onward to his goal.

When a red and white helicopter comes into view, Oxerion takes note of the witches' presence. He stops, lifts his bouldering head high into the sky, and blows smoke out his nostrils; a snarl forms on his snout. A vehicle on the ground comes to a halt below the helicopter and draws Oxerion's attention. Two women jump out and walk toward him with slow strides. He disregards their presence for the moment and focuses on the witches' aircraft hovering out of his fire's reach but close enough that he hears its horn blaring.

"Alright…we've got his attention," Walter says. His nervous breath is clear in everyone's headset.

Kevin nudges Katarina. She recites the spell with her bottom lip trembling. "Encased in fire and ice…"

Upon hearing the child witch's voice, Oxerion releases a roar matching that of three thousand lions bellowing in synchrony. He takes one hop before pouncing toward them with his snout reaching upwards into the sky, opened wide enough to swallow the helicopter whole. Walter maneuvers a narrow escape and lowers the chopper back to a level position away from the dragon. Everyone on board screams and nearly vomits. Katarina's head falls limp as she faints in her seat, the intense jerking motion of the turn having rendered her unconscious.

Just as Oxerion falls back to earth, Patricia shouts a spell and directs her hands toward the desert ground to create a fissure wide enough to entrap his feet. She compresses the gravel and grabs hold of the surrounding pebbles to further encase him. The ground quakes as he fights against their magic, knocking Patricia and Regina off their feet.

Oxerion roars at the two witches. "You!" he says through nasty growls as he recognizes Patricia's face.

"That's right. You know who I am." Patricia stands up tall though her body is still weak from the spell. "Come and get me."

"Don't taunt him," Regina says, stepping backwards and glancing at the helicopter. She lifts boulders from afar and slams them into Oxerion's shoulders and back like a pile driver, pushing him further down into the gap. The fighter pilots follow Regina's lead and release their artillery at the dragons. She wedges him deeper into the earth, trapping him with stone.

Oxerion flaps his flightless wings to no avail, cursing Baronyx and Pterones for his weakness. Flexing his back muscles even harder, Oxerion hopes to create momentum that will propel his body upwards and out of the trap.

Patricia doesn't hear anything over the speakers. She whips out her handheld radio. "What's wrong?"

Walter replies, "Katarina fainted."

Gustavo unbuckles himself and crawls into the rear of the cabin to reach for a red bag below their seats. When he unzips it, he reveals a set of medical implements and plastic envelopes filled with creams, fluids, and powders. He pulls out a blue bottle and unscrews the top. Kevin holds Katarina's head upright. When Gustavo passes the bottle a few times under Katarina's nose, she wakes up.

"Do you know where you are Kat?" Gustavo asks.

Katarina nods, blinking wildly.

"Do you remember the spell?"

"Yes!" The whites of her eyes grow as the realization of the moment hits her. "The spell! Encased in fire and ice…To sleep you will be…"

Upon hearing the words once more, Oxerion forces his entire body up and releases himself from the crack in the earth. He hurls a breath of fire at the two witches on the ground and streams the flames up toward the witches' presence in the air.

Both Regina and Patricia wave their hands to create an invisible shield to ward off Oxerion's attack. They bend down to their knees, unaccustomed to the massive strength of the magical giant, and tuck their heads in as their shield protects them from the flames.

Several jets zoom by, releasing rockets at Oxerion's head and neck to interrupt his attack on Patricia and Regina. The explosions create a thick smoke to block his view, but it doesn't interfere with his mystical senses. He knows exactly where the two witches are.

He redirects his flames toward the helicopter, and Walter dances around in the sky once more. Oxerion takes another leap toward them, coming hazardously close, but this time Baronyx appears from behind and keeps Oxerion's snout from touching the blades. As the two beasts fall to the ground, Oxerion sprays fire towards Patricia and Regina. They raise their arms again to keep the flames from reaching before dropping to their knees from exhaustion.

Walter brings the chopper back to level flight. The cabin is quiet as everyone watches the dragons wrestle. Clouds of dust rise from the scene as Baronyx pulls Oxerion back several hundred feet from where Patricia and Regina are standing. He lifts the black dragon into the air and flings him back westward from where they came.

"That red dragon is definitely on our side," Walter says.

"It doesn't matter," Kevin shouts. "We have to get out of here."

"No." Jasmyn says. "Baronyx doesn't want to harm us. He may know how to stop Oxerion. We have to talk to him. He might know something we don't."

"I doubt he will sacrifice his brother's life."

"No, but maybe he knows how we can control Oxerion. Katarina and I have both read the spell; we've both opened and closed the box, and nothing is working." Jasmyn stares out the window in the direction of the two dragons. "We have to try something else." Jasmyn grimaces as she remembers the visions the black dragon implanted in her mind. "Maybe if we can get into their heads, the way they got into mine—"

"You know," Katarina says, "in one of Patricia's memories, I can see Nana staring at a dragon, like in a staring contest. They just keep looking at each other. Maybe they were communicating!"

Jasmyn's eyes widen. "Maybe the communication goes both ways." She grabs Katarina's hand. "We have to try to make the dragons believe they are not here. Make them believe they're somewhere else, like—"

"Back on their mountain? Back with other dragons?" Katarina interrupts, recalling one of Patricia's memories.

"Yes!"

"And then what?"

After glancing at her father, who narrows his eyes and nods quickly, Jasmyn says, "We can try to get them to…leave the desert and go somewhere far away. Get away from here."

"Then Baronyx can be safe?"

"Yes." Jasmyn swallows hard, forcing a smile. "Then Baronyx can be safe."

Jasmyn and Katarina concentrate. Katarina thinks about the *Book of Whispers* and its pages full of drawings, stories, and spells. She reviews the pictures in her head searching for clues. Jasmyn considers how her empathic sense came to her naturally, and how they both released the dragons with barely any effort on their part. Jasmyn presses her eyelids tightly. *Come on, Nana. Come on. How do I make them see what I see? I know Kat and I must have this gift. If there was ever a gift to give, this is the one.*

A few seconds pass and Jasmyn is bombarded with images of the Isle of Enid: green mountains, glittering ocean, and stony shores upon which waves crash. The visions her ten-year-old mind saw when her grandmother told stories rush back to her.

She remembers the ancient, tree-lined cliffs where rituals took place, the sorceress's maiden dresses and how they flapped in the winds on the top of the mountains, and how the dragons would cast their shadows across the sea, shadows so large that it appeared they would sprout into giant aquatic creatures and leap from the waters.

As her childhood imagination replays itself in her mind, Jasmyn realizes her grandmother had put the visions there the way she is hoping to implant her vision into Baronyx's memory. *These are your memories, Nana, your visions. All this time I thought I was making it up, and it was you all along. Why didn't you say anything?*

A tear finds its way down Jasmyn's cheek as she mentally pushes her imagery toward Baronyx.

~ ~ ~

"You will not kill those children!" Baronyx growls down at his tired, battered brother. His wings cover a diameter so large they create winds strong enough to ward off the news helicopters following the apocalyptic scene.

Oxerion struggles to rise to his feet. He releases a screeching whimper like that of an injured dog. "You are the lowest of all of us dragons! You betray your brothers by helping the enemy, and now you are trying to kill me!"

"You killed Pterones!"

"Pterones was weak."

"He was our brother!"

"You must see that he would have been the death of us. You and I...we are strong. We are mightier than those two child witches."

Baronyx lifts his wings and allows gravity to shoot him

straight into the center of Oxerion's chest. His claws tear into the iron-tough flesh, producing a crackling noise that could only mean Oxerion's chest bones are caving in. With his anger guiding his actions, he raises his shoulders and stomps one more time. "It will be hell, either in this world or in their prison." He roars upwards toward the dozens of choppers, searching for the pull from the one carrying Agatha's kin. He roars, "What are you waiting for? Send us back to your prison! Send us back to hell!"

After two heartbeats, Baronyx finds himself staring down at an old woman resembling Agatha standing on a sharp white stone that juts out from the side of a tree-covered mountainside. It's the same cliff where Finna showed him how to fly, where Agatha and Finna would spend hours talking to him about love, family, and loyalty.

Standing close to the cliff's edge, she raises her right hand toward Baronyx's heart. Her lips curve upward, tenderly, and her eyebrows crease in sorrow.

"Agatha?" He stares down upon his old mother and bows his head in shame, his heart breaking at the sight of her, of the last human who loved him, who had true faith in him. Leaning his neck forward, he allows her hand to palm his rough skin. "Please forgive me. Please forgive me and my brother."

"I forgive you, Baronyx. I do not blame you. But I need your help with Oxerion."

In his mind, Baronyx sees Agatha standing along the mountain ranges of their home island, Oxerion's chest secure under his enormous feet. He presses downwards toward Oxerion's spine, holding back the seductive temptation to crush his brother's killer. "Do not ask me to kill Oxerion. Please. Send us back to your prison."

"We...*I* am unable to cast the spell."

Baronyx snivels and digs his paw deeper into Oxerion's

chest, causing him to cry in pain. "He is the only brother I have left. If I kill him, I will be alone."

Agatha shakes her head to the side and mutters to herself. Baronyx doesn't try to listen, praying silently that she comes up with another solution. Then, suddenly, Pterones appears at the mountain's summit, behind Agatha, looking down the other side of the peak. He flaps his green wings and lifts off toward the horizon. When Baronyx sees his dead brother fly away peacefully toward the sun, he releases a low chuff.

"I can bring back Pterones. I can bring back your brother if you kill Oxerion."

While watching his brother's serene silhouette glide left and right across the Northern Sea, Baronyx drills his claws deeper into Oxerion's torso. His eyes never leave Pterones, taking in his graceful flight form, his whimsical twists and fanciful loops in the air. As the bones underneath Oxerion's skin crumble down, Baronyx sees Pterones blow streams of fire into the reddening sky, cutting off the sunset's rays and creating clouds of smoke in the air.

Other dragon silhouettes appear, flipping, diving, and roaring in playful flight. Dozens of dragons jump out of the waters up toward the puffs of smoke and dive right back into the freezing sea. They fly effortlessly in the twilight sky.

"Take me back to how it once was, Agatha," Baronyx begs as he feels his paws flatten Oxerion's body. He wails out toward the images of his brothers, toward what could be. "It is done. Please…please…take me back."

The scene before him vanishes, and Baronyx finds himself alone in the dry desert standing over Oxerion's dead body. He slumps to the ground next to his brother's corpse as his madness takes hold.

~ ~ ~

"I had to do it, Kat," Jasmyn says as she consoles her sobbing little sister.

"We didn't have to lie to him," Katarina shouts, crying. "He never lied to us."

"I'm sorry Kat, I—"

"No, you're not! You didn't have to create all those other dragons. You didn't have to give him hope. You tricked him. You betrayed him!" Katarina quickly unbuckles herself to climb onto her father's lap for an embrace. She buries her head into his neck as he and Gustavo urge her to get back into her seat.

"It was the only way he would kill Oxerion. And if I knew a way to make Baronyx kill himself, I would do that too. I want this to end. I want us all to go home and forget any of this ever happened!"

Without warning, Walter dips to the right to avoid flames aimed at the helicopter. As Walter shouts into his headset, several military planes fire artillery at the red dragon in the hopes of slowing him down and allowing Walter to escape. Walter pushes his chopper as much as he can, but Baronyx's wings are faster, and his resolve is absolute.

The fluctuating motion nauseates everyone in the helicopter cabin as Walter maneuvers away from streams of fire. Katarina's small frame slips out from her father's hold, and she screams as she bounces against the walls of the helicopter cabin. As her little sister clings to life from a bar just three feet in front of her, Jasmyn unbuckles her seat belt to grab hold of Katarina. She pulls her little sister into her lap and fumbles with her seat belt as the helicopter jerks left and right.

A fighter plane slams against Baronyx's wing and explodes, sending a metal object flying into the side door of the chopper. The impact forces the helicopter door to slide wide open next to the two sisters. A wind thrust whips Katarina out of the helicopter. Two seconds later, she is followed by Jasmyn. Baronyx does not see the two witches fly toward the ground and continues his pursuit of the helicopter.

Regina and Patricia follow the chase in their truck. They watch in horror as Katarina and Jasmyn plummet to the desert surface. Patricia lifts her arms and cradles the two young witches in a cushion of air before they hit the ground, slowing their descent drastically but not completely. She lands them as gently as possible given the trajectory and speed with which they were traveling.

But Patricia's magic isn't enough; her reaction comes too late. Having been sucked first from the helicopter cabin, Katarina slaps the ground twice before rolling onto her back. She lies on the desert floor as Jasmyn tucks and rolls as if she had been skydiving with a parachute. Jasmyn rushes to her sister's battered body and examines her arms that bend awkwardly at the elbows. Bone protrude through her pants from both of her shins. Blood and dirt stain everything.

"No. No. No!" Her trembling fingertips wipe the blood and dirt from Katarina's forehead, tracing her jagged cheekbone down to her jawline and finally resting on top of her chest. Her baby sister's heart beats slowly underneath her bare palm. "Don't take her away from me. Please, please take me. Don't take her. Take me! Take me!"

"Mommy," Katarina whispers, blood filling her mouth.

"It's me, Jaz. I'm right here, Kat. I'm right here."

"I want Mommy," she whimpers. Her bruised eyelids remain closed.

"Mommy's on her way," Jasmyn says, trying to calm her sister's cries. "Stay awake. Don't go to sleep. Remember, you are the strongest little girl I know. Mommy will be so proud of you. I am so proud of you."

"Mommy…" Katarina sobs weakly.

After a few moments, Katarina's whimpers stop.

"No, Kat. No! You have to stay awake."

"I see Nana," Katarina says as the corner of her bloody lip curves upwards. "It's really her."

"I can't do this without you. Stay awake! I need you to stay awake. Do you hear me? I need you. I need you!"

"She looks just like you, Jaz," Katarina whispers before a cough produces red spit that trickles out of her mouth and runs down the side of her face. Her heart stops beating, her face relaxes, and the last breath of air leaves her broken body. Jasmyn's stomach contracts, and she sobs, cursing out loud, shouting questions into the air until her voice is hoarse. "Why? Why did you do this to us, Nana?"

The Humvee skids to a stop behind Jasmyn. The soldier in the vehicle takes an emergency bag to Katarina and begins probing, poking, and injecting her with fluids while talking into the microphone in his helmet. With her eyes locked on her dead baby sister, Jasmyn stands up and walks backwards from the scene.

Regina tries to revive Katarina with her enchantments, but after a minute she touches her forehead, then her heart, and sits back on her knees and cries. The soldier backs away and reports Katarina's death to the base.

With her mouth agape and tears flowing down her face, Patricia walks over to Jasmyn and cradles her jaw with both her hands. "Oh Jasmyn…"

Jasmyn slaps her hands away. "Don't touch me! Don't—" Jasmyn's eyes glow crimson red as she stares straight ahead past Patricia, past the jeep that brought Regina and Patricia to her, and into the far distance.

"Jasmyn, look at me." Patricia inches closer and studies Jasmyn's face. She grabs her shoulders and shakes her body. "Talk to me, Jasmyn. Talk to me!"

Regina runs to Patricia's side. "Baronyx is turning back." She glances at Jasmyn. "What's happening?"

"I don't know. We have to keep Baronyx busy until Jasmyn comes around."

Baronyx's roar reaches Patricia's ears, "We're running out of options."

18

THE PASSAGE

Gazing out over the edge of a steep cliff to the ends of the Northern Sea, Jasmyn gasps. Eager stars twinkle in the dusk until the sky stretches to the setting sun hovering right above the horizon. The serene rhythm of a crashing shoreline fills the air as large, slow-moving waves slam against abandoned boulders at the base of the mountain. A gentle gust of wind picks up Jasmyn's dark auburn hair away from her face, sending it whipping back behind her. It brushes her eyelashes, causing her eyes to close, and caresses the skin around her neck.

I must be dead; this must be heaven. The shoreline resonates with slamming water, as if supporting her revelation. *I don't deserve to be in heaven.*

"Jasmyn," a strange but familiar voice says behind her, away from the cliff's edge.

She turns around to find a young woman with long, wavy auburn hair standing in a cerulean blue frock laced with golden trim at the neckline and wrists. Jasmyn notices the same pattern on her own wrists and chest. "Who are you?"

Her smile fails to put Jasmyn at ease. "I'm Agatha, your grandmother."

Jasmyn swallows. "My grandmother is dead."

"Yes, I am. I am dead, in the natural sense, but I still live within you."

"I'm going crazy then. Is that what this is?"

"Patricia touched you, as she did Katarina, and that

triggered the induction into our coven. But…something is in the way. We are at an impasse. What you see is here is just the beginning."

The scent of forestry mixed with salty air tickles Jasmyn's nose. She scans the mountain all the way up to the towering summit and back down to the flat base of the ocean. "Where are we?"

"We are on the Isle of Enid. This is my birthplace, and the birthplace of our coven."

Jasmyn narrows her eyes. "Nana died an old lady. If you're Nana, why are you so young? I've never seen Nana this young."

The woman smiles again. "Most of my immortal life was in this form, at this age, for three hundred years. These are the years that you are not aware of, the truths I kept from you and the rest of the family, the stories that sound like myth but are as true as the pain you feel for Katarina's death."

A stiff frown appears on Jasmyn's face. "Don't talk about Kat."

The woman nods, folds her hands and tilts her head downward, ruefully.

A few silent seconds pass before Jasmyn asks, "What do you mean we are at an impasse?"

"It appears, after everything that has happened, your heart is shielded. You are not allowing the induction to continue."

"I'm not doing anything."

The gentle expression on the woman's face mimics that of Nana, but Jasmyn doesn't accept the coincidence as proof. "It seems as if you are not, but subconsciously you are. Even now, as we discuss who I am, and Ka-" she pauses, "you are defensive. You don't believe my answers, though I am speaking the truth."

"I'm not defensive. I just…" Images of Katarina lying on

the ground covered in blood and bruises cloud Jasmyn's thoughts. The last thing she remembers is Katarina dying in her arms, hearing her last breath blow out between her swollen lips.

The woman clears her throat and disrupts Jasmyn's spiraling train of thoughts. Her blue frock brushes against the cliff's edge, rustling shards of grass poking through scattered gravel. She walks toward the other edge of the cliff's rock platform, peeking over, and raises her eyebrows. "That's a long way down, don't you think?"

Jasmyn looks at the ocean and follows the path of the waves to the rocky shores. "None of it is real, is it? This is all in my head."

"Do you smell the saltiness in the sea air? Can you feel the wind riding the current as it drives water into the coastline? You can hear the sound of waves battering ancient rocks. Who is to say that it isn't real, simply because it's in your head?"

Unable to come up with a rebuttal, Jasmyn wrinkles her forehead and looks toward the ocean. A barrage of gory images flashes before her eyes. She presses her lids shut to focus in on them, absorbing their unalterable meaning. She imagines herself on the floor, with her arms broken and her face beaten, dead instead of Katarina. *Why couldn't it be me lying there?*

"I know what you're going through, Jasmyn."

She shoots her eyes open and lowers her voice in response, nearly growling at the woman. "You have no idea what I'm going through."

The woman straightens her stance and lifts her chin, inhaling deeply. "I knew the envy that boiled inside of you, the resentment you had toward your sister these past eight years. I felt the putrid jealousy that made you retreat into a solitary lifestyle. Your hate, your anger, was directed at your parents and sometimes at me."

Jasmyn's mouth opens, but she says nothing. She closes it and presses her lips into a solid, stiff line.

"But I also felt how worried you were for Katarina on her first day of school, when she thought everyone would tease her for being so small and wearing thick glasses. I remember how you talked to her about strength and independence, telling her she didn't need anyone's approval. I remember how you taught her how to ignore the mean kids, and how to confuse bullies by walking away as if she didn't care, as if they had no effect on her. I even remember how you followed her to school those first few weeks, making sure no one bothered her."

Jasmyn swallows hard as the memory comes to her.

"When she needed you, you were there for her."

"She needed me so many more times after that, and I never—"

The woman holds up a hand to cut Jasmyn off. "I recall how you would stare at your parents longingly as they would tickle or play with Katarina in the backyard. Whenever Kevin would call Katarina his princess, a hundred spikes would jut out of you in all directions, and sometimes they'd land on me. I knew you ached for your parents' love, for their worry, for any form of consideration, and I knew you suffered when you only received absence or indifference. Your parents didn't realize this, but, in their defense, you were good at hiding your emotions. Although they didn't know how you truly felt, I knew."

"I took it out on Katarina," Jasmyn says, her voice trailing into a whisper. "I didn't—"

Again, she lifts her hand to stop Jasmyn from finishing her sentence. "I can tell you the exact day your regard for me went from sweet to sour. It was when Katarina was eighteen months old, and I was watching you both while your parents took Logan to a basketball game. It rained that day." She looks up at the clouds in the sky and releases a sigh. "Katarina walked into my room and picked up the *Book of Whispers* in her arms, almost dropping it since it was so much bigger than she could manage. We sat in my bed, and I read her a story. That's when you walked in." Agatha sighed once more. "It pained me to know that you believed I didn't love you anymore."

A grimace appears on Jasmyn's face. The coldness of her thoughts back then, the selfishness of the choices she made because she believed no one loved her...her self-loathing becomes so unbearable that she feels nauseated and sits down on a nearby boulder. Tears drip from her eyes as she realizes that only her grandmother could know such things. *Only Nana could have possibly known what I felt.*

The leafy trees at the base of the cliff rustle, lifting Jasmyn's attention from the ground to the woman. Jasmyn sees the sadness in her and is reminded of the somber look she often saw in her grandmother. The familiar expression that Jasmyn used to think was disappointment, even pity, was actually heartache blended with hope.

"Nana," Jasmyn says, swallowing hard to hold back sobs. "I'm sorry, Nana." She stands up, repeats her grandmother's name once more, and embraces her as she has never done before.

"There, there. You have to let it go, Jasmyn. You have to forgive yourself for thinking those things, for feeling that way. You have to realize that your family loves you, just as I know you love them. We are all the products of our circumstances, and we have to do our best to look past the surface and see what lies deep. Sometimes we make mistakes, pass judgment when judgment isn't warranted, and act when we are at our most passionate. And sometimes, we let things try and work themselves out."

She pulls Jasmyn's head back to look into her eyes, and wipes the tears streaming her cheeks. "I had hoped that you would grow out of your jealousy, but... I should have said something to you. I should have told you everything, and then maybe the jealousy would never have been born. All that anger you harbored, all that resentment... I am the one to blame. But now, you have to let it go."

Jasmyn steps back and lowers her head, pressing her swollen eyes shut. "I can't let it go now. Kat's gone. She's dead because of me. It's all my fault."

"Oh, my sweet Jasmyn," Agatha says. "My princess, I am the one who is sorry." She takes a long, deep breath. "Katarina is dead because of me."

The brush behind her whooshes again, giving Agatha a moment of pause, and she looks out toward the sun's brilliant rays. A crisp breeze caresses Jasmyn's face and spreads her tears back and away from her cheeks, almost wiping them dry.

"No sorceress from our coven has ever decided to *not* choose a successor when kin were accessible. After so many years, after so much tragedy and sacrifice, I didn't want to give you or Katarina this burden. I wanted my magic to die with me. But..." She lowers her glance to the grass and huffs. "It seems magic determines its own mortality. It chose you and Katarina. It chose not to die."

With a tender stroke of her hand, Agatha caresses Jasmyn's cheek. "Now, you will inherit all of my power. Since Patricia touched you, her memories of our magic are now yours. She will teach you many things, but there will be a few things you will have to learn for yourself. It was my task to show you, to teach you the magic that is ours only, but this is one task I cannot complete." Agatha smirks as she remembers the last conversation she had with Patricia. "You must be patient with Patricia. Her heart is good even if her actions or words don't always seem like it."

"A lot like me, huh?" Jasmyn asks with arched eyebrows.

"Yes. A lot like you," Agatha replies, grinning. "Before we go any further…"

A loud flock of seagulls race across the sky, drawing Jasmyn's attention away from her grandmother. She follows the flock's flight pattern as it dips left and right and in undulating curves, turning her completely around. When she turns back to face Agatha, she sees a small girl with pigtails and glasses wearing a long white gown with pink and purple daisies that gather at the crumpled trim over her bare feet. Her eyes rise slowly and light up the instant they land on Jasmyn's face.

"Kat?" Jasmyn whispers.

Her springy pigtails bounce when she nods. She looks up at her grandmother. "She's beautiful, isn't she? I told you Nana looks like you."

Jasmyn opens her mouth, but she can't speak. She drops to her knees and cries into her hands, grabbing hold of her dress at her chest, fighting against the wail that is aching to spill out. Unable to find the strength to lift her head and look into the eyes of her baby sister, she remains in a slump. Through uncontrollable sobbing, she begs her sister for forgiveness.

Katarina's tiny hands cradle Jasmyn's chin. "There is nothing to forgive, Jaz. You have to let the past go, all the anger and resentment, just let it float off you like the bad toilet stink it is. It's yucky and sticky. It leaves a bad taste in your mouth, like rotten broccoli."

The imagery makes Jasmyn giggle through her tears, and soon the two girls laugh and cry in each other's arms. With all her might, with all her love and sorrow, and with all the hope she has left, Jasmyn squeezes her arms around little Katarina.

"I always knew you loved me, deep down inside," Katarina says.

"Deep down…like in China?"

She tilts her head and smirks mischievously. "No, right here." Katarina touches Jasmyn's chest, right over her heart.

"It's time," Agatha says as she reaches for their hands and lifts them to their feet. "Ready?"

Jasmyn winks at Katarina, and Katarina winks back. "I'm ready," Jasmyn says.

Agatha places her right hand upon Jasmyn's heart, and her induction continues.

~ ~ ~

"Wake up, Jasmyn!"

Patricia's desperate voice finally breaks through Jasmyn's daze. The crashing sensation of an explosion rattles Jasmyn's bones, jarring her to her knees.

"We have to go!" Gustavo shouts. He picks up Regina in his arms and carries her to the helicopter.

Jasmyn pushes herself to her feet and turns around to find Baronyx lying flat against the desert floor. Her heart nearly sinks out of her body when she sees two soldiers gathering Katarina into a white body bag. Patricia tugs on Jasmyn's shirt to get her to run toward Walter's helicopter. Jasmyn turns back to watch the soldiers carry her sister's remains toward a Humvee, but Patricia pulls her forward. *Not now! Take care of Baronyx. Get out of here!* Jasmyn isn't sure if it's her thoughts or Katarina's voice rambling through her head, but she turns around and jogs alongside Patricia to the chopper.

"What happened?" Jasmyn asks.

"Regina put him to sleep, but Baronyx was too massive for her. She used all her strength to cast the spell. She's not used to using her magic at such magnitudes. I'm not sure how long he'll be asleep."

170

Gustavo climbs into the back of the cabin with Regina. He buckles her into the middle seat and pulls out his emergency kit. Patricia stands at the door, leaning over as if about to throw up.

"Are you hurt?" Jasmyn asks, staring back at Baronyx's mountainous body.

"I'm fine." Jasmyn's presence—the presence of a powerful sorceress—resonates toward her. She stands up and narrows her eyes at Jasmyn. "You're different."

"I am," Jasmyn says, swallowing hard.

Patricia's eyes widen. She searches the helicopter cabin wildly. "Where's the box?"

Gustavo hands it to Patricia.

"We can't read the spell until Baronyx wakes up. He has to be aware of you."

As if on cue, a rumbling groan rises from the red giant. Baronyx twitches his neck and tail against the shards of stone shooting up from the desert floor Patricia created to hold him back.

Patricia and Jasmyn jump into the helicopter's back seat, and Walter takes flight. As the chopper climbs in altitude, Patricia notices the soft purple glow of Jasmyn's aura, similar to the one Agatha used to have. Her wavy auburn hair looks agonizingly familiar, as does the pensive expression on her face. She feels as if she's looking at a younger version of Agatha.

"Why are you staring at me?" Jasmyn asks.

"You suddenly look so much like your grandmother."

The image of a young Agatha appears in Jasmyn's thoughts, standing next to Katarina as they gaze out to the horizon with the wind blowing back the folds of their dresses. Katarina's pigtails flap wildly in the breeze as she turns sideways to look back at Jasmyn. Her cheekbones lift enough to give a hint of smile.

"Kat thought I looked like Nana too." The warm pulsation

Jasmyn feels from Patricia intrigues her. "What are you feeling right now?" Jasmyn asks.

"Melancholy." Patricia adjusts herself in her seat, surprised by her honest response.

Jasmyn nods. "I'm trying to match the emotion with the sensation."

"Ah…it will take some time."

As Walter circles Baronyx's body, Gustavo turns around in his seat. "What's the plan?"

"Jasmyn has to read the spell. If it doesn't work, I'm going to have to use some serious magic to control Baronyx. Which means…"

"You might get sucked into the darkness," Gustavo says.

Patricia nods. "We are immortal in that we don't age and are immune to disease, but we can be killed."

With fear on his face and worn by a loss he has no time to mourn, Gustavo nods. "How will I know?"

Patricia and Gustavo share a moment of sustained eye contact. "I won't look the same as I do now." She swallows hard as she remembers the sight of one of her sister witches turned dark. Her blonde hair shriveled into black, wiry strings, the whites of her eyes turned garnet, and her face darkened from its pearly smoothness to a stony pewter color. "You'll know."

"No," Jasmyn says. The rhythmic beat of the poem appears in Jasmyn's mind. With confidence that has materialized from her grandmother and sister's strength, Jasmyn speaks in a firm, unwavering tone. "It won't come to that. I know exactly what I have to do."

~ ~ ~

The throbbing sensation in his head and the beaten

emotions filling his heart pacify Baronyx. He ignores the blaring horns and the explosions behind him and continues to wallow in his own despair. Buzzing helicopters and fighter planes hover like anxious flies at a picnic, hoping for a moment of opportunity.

He roars up at the sky. "What are you waiting for?"

When he closes his eyes, he imagines black, winged silhouettes gliding gracefully through a sunset sky with their sharp tails trailing lean majestic figures. He hears wails of spirited growls, of dragons calling out to other dragons in a friendly chase, the roars of beasts at play. Green mountainsides blend into stony beaches, with rough ocean waters slapping thousand-year-old rocks along the shoreline. The skies are so clear that the millions of stars shining down upon the world match the millions of splendid sparkles in the deep blue sea.

The rude blare of a horn interrupts Baronyx's daydream. "I don't want to fight. Just send me away. Send me to hell. Put me to sleep," he says in a whine, hoping the witches can hear his thoughts. He presses his eyelids shut once more and releases an agonizing whimper as a happy memory shoves his sorrows to the side. Young Pterones stretches his neck upwards at Baronyx, waiting for instruction, eager to follow his brother's lead. When Baronyx jumps into flight, Pterones darts after him. They fly over the highest peak on their island, poking through cotton clouds, heading upwards toward the midday sun, throwing jovial bursts of fire at one another. The horn blows again, and the memory fades. Baronyx stomps on the ground and roars upwards toward the other helicopters. "Just do it! I will not fight you! Send me to hell, damn you!"

Finna's image appears in Baronyx's mind, walking alongside a cliff. Her beige frock dangles dangerously over the edge as she leans outward to scan the stones at the base of the mountain's shores. "Remember, Baronyx, it is in your nature to

173

fly. You are a dragon." Young Baronyx, barely the size of an elephant, bows his head at Finna and exhales nervously. She recites a spell, presses her lips together, and pushes Baronyx off the cliff. He flaps his wings wildly, but the gust of air spins him out of control. He twists and turns with panic, frightened by the doom racing toward him, shocked by the betrayal. And then, he stretches his wings out and glides upward in flight.

"Baronyx!" Jasmyn shouts in her thoughts from the desert ground less than a hundred feet behind him.

He uncoils his neck and lifts his head to find the helicopters hovering over the gray desert floor surrounding him, with Oxerion's body lying dead a hundred feet away. A small cloud of smoke, followed by a whimpering growl, rises from Baronyx's snout. He lowers his head once more and returns to his reverie.

Patricia pulls Jasmyn's arm to stop their approach. "What's he doing?"

"He's flipping through memories, visions of other dragons, oceans, mountains, from the Isle of Enid. He's waiting for someone to read the spell."

"Then do it."

"Not yet. I have to try something first, for Kat."

Baronyx finds himself facing a cliff along a mountainside where Agatha stands. He gazes at Agatha and moans. "No more tricks. I know you are not Agatha. I know this is all just a dream."

Her disguise fades, and now Jasmyn stands at the cliff's edge. "My name is Jasmyn. I am Agatha's granddaughter."

Baronyx turns away and looks up toward the clouds, his eyes following an invisible pattern in the sky, as if he can still see the silhouettes dancing in the air. "What am I still doing here? Why haven't you entrapped me?"

Jasmyn takes a step closer to the edge, every muscle in

her body tense. "My sister Katarina never wanted to hurt you. She would have wanted me to help you live. Maybe you could go to another part of the world, like the Arctic Circle, somewhere remote where there aren't any people. Katarina would have wanted that."

He snaps his attention back to Jasmyn. "What do you mean she would have? Why do you speak of Katarina in such a way?"

"Because," Jasmyn swallows, "she is dead."

"Young Katarina is dead? How?"

"When you blasted the helicopter with fire, she fell out."

Baronyx turns his head to face Jasmyn. "When you lied to me." Rising to his feet in an aggressive stance, Baronyx growls. "Why did you release us? Why didn't you leave us be? I would at least have had Pterones' thoughts keeping me company. We were used to it all. Why did you have to bring us back?"

"It was a mistake. Kat and I...we—"

"You put all those images in my head. You promised to bring Pterones back." A surge of hate consumes Baronyx as he pictures Katarina's sweet, innocent smile. "Agatha would never have been so cruel."

"I had to stop Oxerion. There was no other way."

"And now young Katarina is dead because of your lies. My brothers are dead because of you. You don't deserve to be Agatha's kin! You deserve to rot in hell!"

He fills his spacious lungs with air and releases a giant flow of fire at Jasmyn.

Patricia puts up a shield to protect herself and Jasmyn from the force of his flames. His mighty paws swing up high in the sky as he prepares to stomp on his adversaries. With her arms still up, Patricia creates another shield just in time to prevent Baronyx from crushing Jasmyn. She falls to her knees with her hands struggling to stay raised above her head, shouting from the excruciating pain as her defense begins to collapse.

With her hands raised above her and out toward Baronyx, Jasmyn begins shouting the spell with authority, the way her grandmother did centuries ago.

"Encased in fire and ice…To sleep you will be…"

Red orbs appear in place of her pupils, and silver light emanates from her frame as her stern tone increases in volume. Her voice is no longer hers, but her grandmother's, and her grandmother's mother, and all the women who have spent their existence passing down the blood that now courses through Jasmyn's veins. Their spirit, their history, their magic reinforces her determination, feeding the menacing strength seeping through her soul.

"Between yesterday and tomorrow…Within here and there…"

Her voice rises to a crescendo as the darkness tempts her. She forms open claws with her fingers, as she sees her grandmother do in Patricia's memory. She flexes her muscles to fight off the intoxicating power luring her in.

"Everywhere   will   be nowhere…Trapped…for…eternity." Baronyx lifts his paws up into the air once more and releases a thunderous roar. Jasmyn opens the box and closes it before his feet slam down on top of her.

Baronyx evaporates into nothingness.

Her arms drop to her side, and she falls to her knees. "I tried, Kat," Jasmyn whispers. "I tried."

~ 19 ~

FAMILY BONDS

Sunlight peeks through the window blinds of the hospital room as a monitor along Regina's bed beeps. A nurse with a dog-tired look on her face marches into the room and over to the machines to press buttons, as if annoyed at the noise. With an uninterested look on her face, the nurse casually checks tubes jutting out of Regina's arms before wrapping her bicep with a blood pressure band.

Patricia walks in carrying a plastic bag with a change of clothes as Jasmyn stretches her back and rubs her neck and shoulders. The nurse and Patricia exchange words at the other side of Regina's bed for a few minutes before the nurse leaves.

"The wake should be happening right about now," Jasmyn says.

"You should be there."

The sweet image of Katarina on the Isle of Enid appears in Jasmyn's mind. "I don't want to be there. I've already said my goodbye to Kat."

Patricia desists when Jasmyn lowers her gaze. *Jasmyn is doing the one thing she knows how to do best—hiding her true emotions and her darkest fears behind a fortified exterior, almost to the point of seeming apathetic. It takes one to know one.* She looks at Regina, sleeping. *I hope you wake up soon. We need some of your hippie sunshine and rainbows.*

The hospital room door swings open and Brian peeks inside, holding a tray with two cups of coffee and a brown paper bag. He places the tray down on the rectangular swivel table at the end of the bed, away from the couch where Jasmyn sits. He hands Jasmyn a bagel with cream cheese, Patricia a whole wheat bagel with butter, and then takes a bite of his pumpernickel with extra cream cheese. He sits down next to Jasmyn on a plastic chair he dragged in from the hallway.

Closing her eyes, she allows the smell of freshly ground coffee to overcome the sterile hospital odors. The familiar flavor gives her an optimistic sense of normalcy, but the bittersweet taste fades as her mind sinks back into the dark abyss of recent days, splashing into the thick waters of self-loathing and regret.

"I spoke to your brother last night," Brian says with a mouth full of bagel.

"What did he say?"

"He asked if I could send him updates on how you're doing, at least until you decide to go home, if that's okay with you."

Jasmyn sighs. "I might not go home for a long time."

"I know."

"I mean…I'm not just waiting for Regina to wake up. I might not go for a long while after that."

"I know," Brian says. He takes another bite of his bagel and sits back in his chair. "He understands why you didn't go home for the funeral."

"Does he?"

"He asked me to tell you that…no one blames you for anything."

The sharp knives Jasmyn felt against her skin, coming from her parents and Logan when they were all reunited afterwards gave a different impression. It was the reception Jasmyn expected, but it still pained her to receive it, especially from her brother. She says nothing in response to Logan's message; she swore never to speak or think negatively of her parents again. They lost their daughter because of her actions; whatever their crimes against her, they've paid them in full and then some.

"Some people," Patricia pauses as she turns from Regina to face Jasmyn and Brian, "need to place blame on someone else for their loss in order to move on. It's a healing mechanism. Don't take it personally. Time will prove them wrong."

"Will it?" Jasmyn asks, darting a glare at Patricia.

"You know this isn't your fault, Jasmyn."

"Not entirely, but I was the catalyst that put everything into motion. If I hadn't destroyed the box, or eavesdropped on Kat and Logan's conversation that night, or maybe if I wasn't so jealous and selfish and hungry for revenge, then maybe…"

Jasmyn closes her eyes and leans back on the couch. She takes a deep breath, concentrating on Katarina's wide eyes and buck-toothed grin. A warm cocoon-like sensation enwraps Jasmyn's limbs as Patricia's and Brian's sympathy for her compresses her body, making her feel like she is bundled in a thick blanket. She flexes her muscles, fighting off the soporific effect of their pity.

Brian clears his throat. "Logan also asked if you need him to send you anything: clothes, money, or anything from your grandmother's room."

"Tell Logan to box up all of Agatha's things," Patricia says as she gazes upon Regina. "They need to be stowed away, out of easy reach."

With a nod, Brian begins typing up an email.

"Did my parents send a message?" Jasmyn asks, looking down at her hands.

A loud gulp emanates from Brian's throat as he prematurely swallows a half-chewed piece of bagel. "He didn't mention your parents."

"Give them time," Patricia says without looking at her.

From the short wooden table behind the couch, Jasmyn picks up the *Book of Whispers* and flips the worn pages slowly, carefully, trying to read them as details of the last few days traverse her mind like rowboats spinning in a whirlpool. One thought in particular repeats itself—*Kat is dead, and there is nothing I can do about it.*

~ ~ ~

The day after the burial, Logan finds himself waking up in the living room in his pajamas at eleven in the morning. Jinx's head pops up next to the couch the instant Logan stands up, his tail wagging and waiting for play. Logan bends down to rub Jinx's hairy head and inches his way up the stairs toward his room. He walks past Katarina's room and finds his mother asleep in her bed under Katarina's pink and purple covers and his father asleep on Katarina's chair with his head tilted back and his mouth wide open. Several empty tissue boxes lie abandoned throughout the room. He shuts Katarina's bedroom door gently.

He notices a sparkle shining through the open crack of Jasmyn's bedroom door, drawing his interest, pulling him toward her room and urging him to look inside. He steps in and finds a mess of clothes on her bed, shoes and socks on the floor, and scattered papers on her desk. Nothing unusual stands out in her room except a small, brown leather book with twine looping around a metal knob as a closure. Jasmyn's journal has a crisscross pattern etched into the leather cover. A red satin bookmark nudged in the middle of the book at the spine attracts Logan's gaze, inviting him to take a peek.

Logan is not a nosy person, nor a suspicious brother who

sneaks around his sister's room, but he is curious about what is inside Jasmyn's journal. He hesitates, wondering if he really wants to see the inner demons he knows his sister possesses. To read about her anger toward Katarina, now that Katarina is dead, might be unbearable.

For the first few hours after Katarina's death, Logan could not even look at Jasmyn. He felt her selfishness and jealousy triggered the events that led to his baby sister's death. But, since then, he's had time to see it from his sister's point of view. As much as he cried over Katarina's death, he knows Jasmyn's suffering is far greater, possibly even stronger than his parents' pain. Even Brian expressed concern over Jasmyn's thinly veiled stoicism, which he believes is an attempt to cover up her deep depression. Knowing his sister blames herself for Katarina's death, Logan fears he might lose his older sister as well, and the thought brings a resentful tear to his eye.

He places the book back down on the table exactly as he found it. With curious eyes, he studies Jasmyn's room, hopping from the miniature clay statues she sculpted to her collection of colorful paints and pastels she used to produce the artwork hanging on her walls. Jars full of sculpting tools and paint brushes glimmer from the rays of sunlight streaking through her window. Along her wall are various frames of different colors and sizes holding photos, sketches, and collages made from magazine paper. On her bedside table, he spots a small photo of Jasmyn making a funny face. He picks up the white frame and pulls it in for a closer inspection. The self-taken shot with her arms reaching toward the sides of the photo shows her sticking her tongue out to the side while crossing her eyes. Logan smiles for a moment before seeing the brown leather journal on the table behind her in the background.

His curiosity no longer taking a back seat to his integrity,

Logan turns back around to Jasmyn's desk and picks up the journal. Never before in his life has he felt the need to know what Jasmyn thinks as he does right now. Maybe it's his little sister's absence or the guilt he feels for having hated Jasmyn for those few hours after Katarina died or the unusual feeling of not really knowing anything about the only sister he has left. Whatever it is, he needs to know something, anything, about Jasmyn. Since she won't talk to him or answer his emails or even send a message through Brian, Logan has no other way to know more about her.

As a curator handles a rare and valuable piece of art, Logan carefully unwinds the twine from the knob and unlocks the journal. He lets the book fall open in his hands to where the red satin bookmark is tucked, on a blank page ready for Jasmyn to enter her latest thoughts. With gentle finger strokes, he turns back the pages to the beginning of the last entry, dated the day his grandmother died.

April 28th – Time: Noon

Nana died earlier this morning. I had a dream about her last night. She was walking along a beach, and she was young. She called my name, waved to me, and started walking toward the water. I was a baby, and I didn't want to go, but she kept calling me. Then I woke up, and I could have sworn someone was saying my name. I got out of bed and went to Nana's room. It felt strange, like her room was alive. I didn't touch her, but I knew she was dead. It's a sad, sad day in our house.

Mom and Dad have been busy with the funeral all morning. I hear Logan in Kat's room. She's been crying a lot, and he's been cheering her up. I've been crying too, but mostly sleeping.

Time: 11 PM

I can't believe Logan and Kat went through Nana's things without me. She's my grandmother too! And Nana's dragon medallion, of all things! I have loved that necklace since I was little, ever since Nana told me about it. I have to write the story down before I forget the details. Maybe, when Kat's older, MAYBE I'll share it with her. Until then, it will be my story.

The Dragon Medallion
(As told to me by Nana when I was a kid)

There was once an immortal witch named Finna who witnessed the demise of her coven at the hands of the Foreman Clan. This band of evil sorcerers set out to enslave and torture the people of the Isle of Enid and kill all the witches and their families. But the clansmen didn't know that this particular sorceress had the power to go back in time, back into her lifetime as a younger self. When the end was near, she used this power and went back in time to warn her coven of the oncoming doom. She created powerful dragons to defend the island against the Foreman Clan, and she saved the lives of the witches and the people of the Isle of Enid.

But time traveling comes at a price. Before she used her magic, Finna had a family— a husband and two small children. She had to alter her life in order to save her coven, and in doing so she never crossed paths with her husband again and therefore never had the children she remembers loving so dearly. Once his time in this world passed, Finna created this dragon medallion as a reminder of the reason she sacrificed her family, and the consequences of using her power. The power of traveling back in time is final and cannot be undone, and what is lost in doing so may never be found again.

The End

I loved that last part. "The power of traveling back in time is final and cannot be undone, and what is lost in doing so may never be found again." Those were the exact words Nana used whenever she told me the story. She was such a good storyteller. It's been years since she's read me a story. Now, I'll never hear her voice again.

I'm sorry Nana, if I was ever mean to you. I wish I could hear you tell me a story the way you used to. I love you. I really hope you knew I loved you.

Logan closes the book slowly, winds the twine three times around the knob, and stuffs the journal under his armpit. He pulls out his cell phone to dial Brian's number, but his voicemail recording greets him on the line.

The doorbell rings. Logan yells out to his parents, "I'll get it."

He tries Brian's number once more without luck.

The doorbell rings again.

With his phone still in his hand, cursing under his breath, Logan heads down the staircase to answer the door. *Nana had that power, I can feel it in my bones. And if Nana had that power, then Jaz definitely has it.*

~ ~ ~

While Logan explores his sister's journal, halfway across the world, Caderyn prepares for travel. When he pulls the zipper to close his vinyl suitcase, a chirping sound draws his attention toward the sky outside his window. He studies the clouds floating effortlessly across the atmosphere and sighs as he remembers the last time he saw any of the sorceresses from the Isle of Enid. It's been centuries.

"Our flight leaves in three hours. It is at least an hour to Lisbon Airport. We need to leave soon," Kean says as he lights up a slim cigarette and sits down on the cushion of the rustic wooden rocking chair. He straightens his white button-down shirt and black sleek slacks and removes a tiny ball of lint from his thigh, tossing it carelessly out the window.

"Did you send Arsen to find the witch?" Caderyn asks, looking back at Kean as the floor creaks with each row of the rocking chair.

"Yes. He arrived in San Francisco in the early morning. As soon as he gathers the witch's artifacts, he will be on a return flight here, most likely by the evening hour. Have you seen the news footage of her family?"

"No," Caderyn says and returns his gaze to the clouds.

Decades ago, Caderyn gave up the pursuit of power, like a long overdue vacation, and made an effort to live peacefully in the coastal town of Cascais, Portugal. The wives and mistresses of international dignitaries, and the lonely wives and widows of billionaires, gave him enough entertainment. When he wasn't socializing, he tended to his hobbies of playing the violin, strumming classical guitar pieces, and reading every book he could possibly get his hands on. These past few decades have been the most tranquil time of his existence, and it ended abruptly when he saw the news about the Gregorn Dragons attacking San Francisco. The seeds of vengeance sprouted once again, and he gathered his brothers, the few he has left, as quickly as he could.

Gazing out the window, Caderyn twists his onyx ring around his ring finger. Of all the luxuries he's had in the world in the past centuries, none compare to his family's onyx ring, except the treasures he may find with Agatha's kin. His clansmen, his ancestors, and his brothers will be avenged.

"You should take a look at this video from the BBC." Kean gives Caderyn a tablet. The reporter displays photos of Jasmyn and her family and a brief summary of their involvement in the chaos, finishing the segment with speculations of sorcery, government secrets, and nuclear experimentation that led to the giant creatures.

186

A photo of Jasmyn fills the screen. Caderyn's lips part when he sees it. "Agatha," he whispers. Suddenly, an onslaught of emotions that have been dormant for centuries bombard Caderyn's calm. He forces his face to remain expressionless, knowing Kean is watching his every move. *There can be no signs of weakness.*

"Not exactly." Kean's eyes narrow as he studies Caderyn's face. Kean swipes his finger across the screen to peruse photos of Agatha's family circulating in the news. "This is her granddaughter, Jasmyn. She's eighteen years old. The other girl, Katarina, was eight—she died in the desert," Kean swipes once more and lands on a photo of Logan. "And this is sixteen-year-old Logan."

A shiver passes throughout Caderyn's entire body as he sees a younger image of himself smiling in the photo. His heart beats strong in his chest, and he breathes slowly to control his heart rate. *He is not your kin. He will take nothing from you!*

"Logan has…an air of you," Kean says cautiously.

Caderyn gives Kean a sideways glare.

After quickly clearing his throat, Kean swipes backwards to the photo of Jasmyn and backs away from Caderyn. "It seems Jasmyn was the one who released the dragons." He sits back down on the rocking chair and takes one final puff from his cigarette before flicking it out the window. "If she is truly Agatha's kin, then…with the Forbidden Consumption, we could go back to before the time the witches of Enid attacked us. Our brothers would no longer be dead, and we could—"

"In all my years in this world, I have never been so mad as to consume a supernatural heart. It is sure passage into the darkness."

"That's not a guarantee." Kean steps back away from Caderyn. His face twists. "Do you still care about Agatha?"

The chirps draw his gaze toward the window once more.

"After everything she has done to you? She killed your clansmen. She destroyed our family. She even killed you!"

"But she didn't kill me, did she Kean?" He walks toward the end of the room, staring at the black marble floor. "And you are talking about eating that child's heart, not Agatha's."

"I'm talking about consuming our enemy in order to gain their power. This child is a full-grown witch. Only Finna's bloodline can perform that time travel incantation." Kean sees hesitation in Caderyn's eyes, in his pacing, in the way he combs his fingers through his jet-black hair. He leans in closer to Caderyn. "It does not matter that Doran disguised himself as you. Agatha was not aware of the trap. Her intention was clear when she slit his throat in cold blood."

He stares out the window as he remembers how his own daughter passed the blade across his neck with calculated precision, without emotion, without reaction as Doran's body slid lifelessly to the ground. Caderyn's eyes moisten; he blinks rapidly and turns away from Kean. *She is not my kin. She is not my family. She is the child of my enemy, a pawn and nothing more.*

Looking side to side, searching for a way to convince his brother, Kean rubs his fists and leans into Caderyn once more. "If the deed is too much for you, it can be done for you. It will be clean, quick, and painless. She won't feel a thing. You could, then, consume her heart, and we could—"

"Enough!" Caderyn's voice rumbles against the concrete walls of his beachfront villa. His eyes glow a fiery red, and a slight wind twirls in the room as he steps toward Kean, forcing him to retreat. "We will get the child witch to give us the dragon that belonged to my ancestors. A live, beating dragon heart is all we need to create an army that no one can defeat."

"And if she refuses to hand over the dragon?" Kean asks boldly, holding his breath, swallowing hard.

Caderyn curls his right hand into an eagle claw. "Then I will take it from her!"

~ End Of Book One ~

ACKNOWLEDGMENTS

One night, I woke up from a dream of a witch on her deathbed about to grant her granddaughters the gift of magic, and upon her death, three dragon eggs fell from the sky. I swear, my dreams are that crazy. Soon after, the first draft of The Box Of Souls was born.

I had completed the first draft in three months. From its inception, the manuscript was all over the place. One afternoon I accompanied an author friend of mine, Yueh Goffin, on her trip to New York City to sell her book to The Strand. During our lunch, I told her my plan, plot, characters, everything about the Family Relics Series. Her advice? "Take your time. Don't rush it. There are a lot of details and you don't want to miss a thing." Thank you Yueh for those wise words. I listened. I took my time with this novel.

I'd like to thank the incredible team at Quill Pen Editorial. A heartfelt thanks to Christabel Barry for helping me develop my story into what it is today. You asked all the right questions. Thanks to Catherine Jones Pane and Stephanie Guido for helping me scoop the tiny bits of fecal matter out of my manuscript during line edits. And thanks to all three of you for all your critiques. I've never enjoyed critiquing as much as I did from you all, even the tough ones. Especially the tough ones.

To Jenny Zemanek, the genius at Seedlings Design Studio, who created the beautiful cover for the first book in the series, I thank thee. To be able to pull *my* ideas out of *my* head and into *her* work – that's true talent. Sometimes, I can't understand what's going on up there.

To my son who is so amazed that mommy's name is on the cover of a book – thank you for being so easily impressed at the age of seven. Thanks to my husband who had no problem eating leftovers and ordering takeout because I constantly forgot about dinner. He may not cook, but he knows all the good eats in town.

A special thanks to my daughter who, after having a tough-yet-successful year in her 8th grade writing course, insists I stop calling myself a stay-at-home mom because, in her own words, "You are writing, and writing is hard work."

And finally, to everyone who chose to purchase my book, thank you a million times over. I hope you enjoyed reading it as much as I enjoyed writing it.

ABOUT THE AUTHOR

Tanya Miranda grew up daydreaming about everything. From human-looking aliens hiding in the government, to witches and dragons skulking in the shadowy corners of her basement, to finding the love of her life running through a hailstorm; her imagination never ceases to create kooky characters in the most bizarre circumstances. Her one true wish is to draw the images that materialize in her head. Until then, she'll continue to put her dreams into stories.

To find out more about the author's writing, visit her at
www.tanyamiranda.com